# GHOST
## STORIES FROM
# MUSSOORIE

**Anmol Jain** was born and raised in Mussoorie. His family is among the oldest in town, residing there since 1901. He is an MBA from a premier institute and, for two decades, has worked as a consultant with international development agencies focusing on climate change and rural livelihoods, particularly in the Himalaya. Author of the critically acclaimed book *Wanderings in the Land of Mist: The Complete Story of Mussoorie,* he also writes for *The Times of India.* He is an inveterate vagabond in his spare time—roaming the mountain slopes, meeting people and indulging in captivating gossip.

Facebook: anmol.jain.77
Instagram: @anmolj_75
Twitter: @im_anmoljain

'I shall hand out free copies of this great book in Rajpur, before the hordes drive up in their pompous SUVs to pollute the peace and quiet of Mussoorie. This craftily scripted book of true ghost stories will scare the scheisße out of them and hopefully they shall flee from our stalking shadows, squeaky hinges and creaking floorboards. Thank you Anmol, for doing us residents of "haunted" Landour this eerie public service.'

—**Victor Banerjee**

# GHOST
## STORIES FROM
# MUSSOORIE

### ANMOL JAIN

RUPA

Published by
Rupa Publications India Pvt. Ltd 2025
7/16, Ansari Road, Daryaganj
New Delhi 110002

*Sales centres:*
Bengaluru Chennai Hyderabad
Jaipur Kathmandu Kolkata
Mumbai Prayagraj

P-ISBN: 978-93-7003-060-2
E-ISBN: 978-93-7003-045-9

First impression 2025

10 9 8 7 6 5 4 3 2 1

*In memory of*
*my dear grandfather, Shri K.P. Jain*
*and father, Shri S.P. Jain*

∞

# Contents

# Foreword

That ghost stories refer to real events is borne out by the fact that they are found in every country and come alive as authentic everywhere only after dark. As a boy growing up in far-away Scotland, when I passed the village War Memorial by day, I walked normally; but at night I always ran past it since it commemorated the departed souls of brave young soldiers killed in battle.

Now, as I drive down to Dehradun from Mussoorie in the morning, I have no care in the world. But driving back in the dark, my foot never leaves the accelerator of its own accord until I reach the safety of the lights of the Kincraig petrol pump. I convince myself this habit is not from fear but common sense. Being alive in the full light of day, the living soul has a distinct advantage over the departed, discarnate soul. But at night, in the dark, the score evens up; for who knows what a dislodged, unhappy soul can get up to?

If you want to know more about the possibilities thrown up on the Mussoorie-Dehradun road in the dark, and the advisability of keeping your foot on the accelerator rather than stop and give a young lady—whose feet point backwards—a lift, read this book written by the compelling pen of Anmol Jain, the local expert on 'ghosties and ghoulies and things that go bump in the night'.

Bill Aitken
March 2025

# Preface

Why is it that hill stations, especially Mussoorie, brim with tales of the supernatural? Do restless spirits truly wander these misty towns, or do idle minds, with time to spare, weave these eerie yarns? Could it be the old British-era houses—crumbling relics of a bygone age, each whispering a poignant tale—that spark such ghostly legends? Or is it the thick fog that drapes the hills, conjuring illusions on dark, desolate nights?

Growing up in the hills, I was steeped in these stories from childhood. They were as much a part of the landscape as the oak trees and winding paths. I'd often catch my grandfather and father murmuring about spirits in hushed, reverent tones.

One memory stands out: my grandfather, leaning toward a friend, his voice low. 'Three English spinsters once lived in this very house,' he said. 'All of them died here, and their ghosts lingered, until we bought the place and held a puja for salvation of their souls.'

From that moment, my younger sister and I saw our home differently. Every shadow held a secret, we would carefully scan all dark corners before venturing into any room.

The long gallery to the washroom became a nightly ordeal; the light switch maddeningly out of reach at the far end. But somehow those countless scary nights passed without any incident!

As we grew older, we'd beg grandfather for more tales. A master storyteller, he'd oblige, spinning chilling accounts of spectral figures and unexplained sounds that echoed through Mussoorie's past. I listened, enthralled, but unconvinced.

Ghosts, I told myself, were figments of imagination. The dense fog, the dark rainy nights, the silhouettes of decaying houses and weathered gravestones—these were enough to unsettle anyone. Add in the local shopkeepers, garrulous and bored during the lean winter months, and you had the perfect recipe for ghost stories. That's what I firmly believed.

Then, more than two decades ago, everything changed. A personal encounter with a ghost—too vivid, too terrifying to dismiss—shattered my scepticism in a single night. That story, one of many you'll find in these pages, marked the beginning of a new reality for me.

Since then I have been in constant fear of ghosts. My son often urges me to watch horror shows on Netflix but I have never obliged him. 'I feel scared of watching horror movies and shows,' I maintain.

'If you can write about ghosts, why can't you watch them?' He asks, grinning.

I will not be truthful if I do not admit that whenever I recall stories about ghosts I shudder to imagine if these ghosts are still lurking around in the town. What if they are watching me write about them, reading every word I write and smiling when I miss some detail?

This book is a collection of haunted stories drawn from Mussoorie's shadowed corners—tales whispered by locals and, in some cases, lived by me. Rooted in true events, they peel back the veil between our world and the unknown.

# The Hitchhiking Chudail

It was a crisp autumn evening as I navigated the winding roads from my office in Dehradun back to Mussoorie. My daily grind, starting with the early morning departure and concluding as dusk painted the sky—occasionally extending into the evening as demanded by the workload—had been a routine for almost a year, ever since I took up a position in an NGO after my studies. My only companion was our family's old blue Maruti.

As I was driving up that evening, I felt a sudden icy chill. 'A bit unusual to be so cold in October... Perhaps it will snow early,' I thought as I pulled up my window and switched on the car's heater.

Within seconds the windshield fogged up, making it impossible to drive on the narrow mountain road. Panic-stricken, I applied the brakes. As soon as the car came to a halt, I turned off the heater and rolled open my window and waited for the windshield to clear.

The sun had completely set by then, allowing the moon to make an appearance. In its dim light I could make out the silvery silhouette of the winding road that stretched a little distance ahead before disappearing from view as it curved towards the right, hidden by trees and rocks.

A few oak trees cast tall shadows on the moonlit road. The only sounds were the rustling of leaves stirred by a gentle breeze and the buzzing of cicadas.

I restarted the car and drove forward. The biting cold made me very uncomfortable, but I dared not switch on the heater as I could not risk the windshield getting fogged up again.

Although there was no vehicle behind me, I don't know why I glanced at the rear-view mirror.

A pair of eyes peered at me from the backseat! Also visible was the outline of a pale face—the face of a young woman. The lips were bright red which slowly parted as a vile grin crept across her face. Before I could react, her icy white fingers reached for my throat, the sharp, red-painted nails resembling a claw.

'Leave me alone, for God's…' The muffled cry barely escaped my throat as my car rammed into the crash barrier by the road.

I woke up with a start, trembling and sweating. 'Thank God it was *just* another dream!' I exclaimed as I tried to regain my composure.

Such nightmares had been haunting me for the past two months; ever since I learnt about the sinister occurrences on this road.

It all started when I gave a lift to two policemen from Kolhukhet (about mid-way between Dehradun and Mussoorie).

Policemen posted at the outpost in Kolhukhet often asked me for lifts as they had to go to Mussoorie to escort the last bus to Dehradun. Yes, you read it correctly—a police escort for the bus!

The year was 2001 and a series of dacoities had occurred on the road—the passengers of two roadways buses and several individuals had been looted. The dacoits would block the road (in those days there was little traffic after 8.00 or 9.00 p.m.), loot the vehicles and flee into the forests below the road.

I have always been a curious and inquisitive person. As per my habit I spoke to several victims of the bus robberies—Mussoorie being a small town, many of them happened to be friends and acquaintances. Rohit—an acquaintance who was a braggart of sorts—was travelling on one of these ill-fated buses to apparently catch the night train to New Delhi. His narration of the ordeal left me and a few other friends in splits.

'I tell you they were amateurs, I could have taken them down easily,' he announced.

'And how would you have done that?' I asked, trying to hide my grin.

'They were four but only one of them had a gun—a country-made pistol—and the pistol wielding leader was a fatso who held it in one hand and kept pulling up his trousers with the other,' Rohit explained.

'The fatso was lucky that I was at the back of the bus. If he had come anywhere near me, I would have pinched the gun from his hand while he was busy keeping his trousers from falling to the ground,' he claimed.

Coming back to our serious discussion about the dacoits, despite repeated incidents the police were unable to nab the culprits. As a countermeasure, a night patrol was started and two policemen from Kolhukhet were deputed to reach Mussoorie in the evening and take the last roadways bus from there. They would get down somewhere on the way and patrol the road all night.

One fateful evening, as I was driving to Mussoorie, I gave a lift to Jogendra and Raman (names changed)—two constables on patrol duty for the night.

As I drove for about two kilometres from Kolhukhet, Raman, who had apparently been on patrol the night before as well, turned to Jogendra in the back seat and pointed outside, 'She was here!'

'And where did you find Sudhir?' asked Jogendra.

'A little higher up on this road.'

That set my alarm bells ringing and I pressed hard on the brake pedal. Raman got a sudden jolt and his 303 rifle, which he was holding in an upright position with its butt resting on the floor, almost collided with the windshield.

'What is the matter with you? Why did you stop the car like this?' Raman growled, his face turning red with anger.

'Brother, what happened to Sudhir?' I enquired sheepishly.

'It's nothing. Please drive,' Raman tried to not sound annoyed.

But after repeated requests his anger subsided, and he reluctantly divulged the details of the events during their previous night's patrol.

Raman started off by mentioning that over the past few months there had been regular reports that a woman was seen in the Chunakhala area at night.

'This woman was seen only by those who were driving alone. And as per the majority of reports, she was seen by those on motorcycles and scooters,' Raman said.

'She is very pretty too! And always seen wearing a tight-fitting jeans and top,' Jogendra butted in.

'Shut up Jogendra, this is serious stuff,' Raman snapped and added that this woman would ask people for a lift.

'Who would refuse to give a lift to a beautiful woman? But they were left in shock and fear as the woman disappeared after travelling a short distance,' he continued.

Jogendra added that several people came to their outpost at night, scared and dumbfounded. He named some people—a few of whom I knew—who had come to the police and reported their creepy experiences with this 'vanishing hitchhiker'. After many such reports, the constables tried to keep a strict vigil in this area during their patrols. But none of them had had an encounter with the woman until yesterday.

Tension was writ large on both their faces. The wind moaned through the trees, its ghostly sighs adding a certain eeriness to the cold autumn evening.

I waited expectantly for Raman to continue narrating his encounter with the woman. He glanced at me, took a deep breath, and began, 'I did not believe in ghosts *or* in this story. But yesterday's creepy incident has left me shocked.'

He narrated that the night before, he and Sudhir had escorted the last bus from Mussoorie, as usual, and had gotten down a short distance after Bhatta village[*] to walk the remaining few kilometres upto Kolhukhet as part of their patrol route.

'You see that road going to the right,' Raman turned and pointed to the Jharipani road a little distance behind our car.

This road branched from the main Dehradun road at Chunakhala and led to Mussoorie via Jharipani. Surrounded by dense forests, it was a very narrow road in those times with little traffic (although the road still remains quite narrow, it is a much-preferred shortcut to Mussoorie now).

'It was around 10.00 p.m. when Sudhir and I reached this spot yesterday. The road was completely secluded and an eerie silence prevailed. In the moonlight we saw a woman standing alone on the roadside, right at the bend where the Jharipani road starts.

'I tried to switch on my torch but it didn't light up! Nevertheless, we rushed towards her in the semi-darkness, fearing that she might be a victim of some mishap. Approaching her, I could make out her profile. She was short—a little over 5 feet in height—wore a pair of tight

---

[*]Travelling from Mussoorie to Dehradun, you first cross Bhatta village—about 7 km from Mussoorie—and travelling 7–8 km further you reach Kolhukhet, a small village where there is a police outpost and a few tea shops. Chunakhala, where the road to Jharipani branches out, falls about mid-way between the two villages.

jeans and a top; her long, un-braided hair fluttered in the gentle breeze. I noticed that she had a pale white face and her lips were covered with a thick coat of lipstick. But her eyes...her eyes...!'

Raman stammered. His face went pale as he stared vaguely outside the car.

'What about her eyes?' I asked eagerly. My voice seemed to wake him from a reverie.

'She had no eyes... Just empty sockets,' he whispered after a long pause.

'What?' I blurted with disbelief, feeling that Raman had been too scared last night and his fear had made him imagine things.

'Yes, she had no eyes!' Raman repeated.

'Her face had a wicked grin as she stared at us through empty sockets. As I stood rooted in fear—my feet trembling, heart pounding against my chest—the woman vanished into thin air.'

However, he said that Sudhir could seemingly still see the woman.

'Sudhir looked dazed. He seemed oblivious of my presence; eyes locked in one direction, he started walking towards the opposite side of the road. Towards the edge that bordered a deep gorge.

'"Sudhir, stop! Sudhir...!" I shouted, somehow managing to gather my wits as I ran towards him.'

Raman narrated that Sudhir had almost reached the edge of the road when he was somehow able to catch hold of him.

'Sudhir struggled wildly to get out of my grip. He was shouting, "*mein aa raha hoon;* I am coming…" until he collapsed in my arms.'

'What happened after that? Did the woman appear again? Where is Sudhir now?' I asked in one breath.

Raman replied that Sudhir was unconscious and did not come to his senses despite a lot of effort.

'Thankfully, the ghost did not appear again. But I had to wait there for nearly half an hour—trembling and chanting the Hanuman Chalisa—until a car came down the road. Sudhir had to be admitted to the hospital. I met him today morning; he is conscious now but not in his senses. "*Woh bula rahi hai;* she is calling me…" he keeps muttering.'

I do not know what took over me as I announced, 'Let's walk to the place where you saw the woman and where Sudhir collapsed.'

I was feeling a bit adventurous since I thought that the tale was a figment of Raman and Sudhir's imagination. Obviously, walking alone at night with stories of hitchhiking ghosts doing the rounds could make one delusional.

'Have you lost your mind?' Raman and Jogendra shouted in unison.

I explained that maybe this ghost woman did not exist. Perhaps the accounts of a few people had scared everyone into imagining similar things.

'Let's go to the place and check—after all, we are

three and you two also have rifles. Isn't it the duty of the police to investigate such matters?' I tried to boost their confidence.

In hindsight, it was a foolhardy thing to do. But sometimes, we end up doing things on the spur of the moment which we may regret later.

After arguing for a few minutes, both of them agreed to check the place once.

'Ok. We will quickly go to the place where Raman saw the ghost and then across the road to where he caught Sudhir. But after that we will leave immediately. No further arguments about this,' Jogendra said with finality and looked at Raman, who reluctantly nodded.

The three of us got down from the car and walked back towards the Jharipani road. I would be lying if I do not admit that I had some butterflies in my stomach.

Raman switched on his torch—which thankfully worked today—and pointed it towards the side of the road. He and Jogendra were pale and tense, their eyes glued ahead trying to pierce through the darkness.

'See! There is nothing here, Raman. You and Sudhir must have imagined things yesterday,' I remarked, a bit emboldened by now.

Raman let out a deep sigh, looked at me and nodded. He seemed a bit relieved.

'Ok, let's quickly go across the road where Sudhir had collapsed and then let's go back. I am not getting good vibes standing here at this forsaken spot,' Raman said as he led us across the hill road to its edge, which bordered a deep gorge. It was a drop of about 50 feet from this point.

'See there's nothing...' My words got stuck in my throat as the low wail of a woman emanated from the gorge below. We stood paralyzed with fear as the pitch of the wail continued to increase, until it turned into a bloodcurdling laughter.

'*Mere paas aao... Mere paas aao* (come to me)...' A demonic voice beckoned us from below the road.

Panic surged through me. I glanced at Raman and saw that he was trembling. His eyes were wide and fixated, and his mouth was agape in a silent scream.

In the middle of this terror, Jogendra somehow managed to gather his wits. He tried to shout but could only croak a single word: '*Run!*'

With that, the three of us turned and ran up the road towards my car. The constables with their rifles were finding it difficult to match my pace. The raucous laughter followed us, growing louder every passing second.

I have never run so fast in my life! Reaching the car, despite my trembling hands, I somehow managed to insert the key in the lock and opened the doors. All three of us dove into the safety of the car.

The laughter had died down by then. Horrified and out of breath, we sat motionless in the car. Despite the cold, sweat trickled down my forehead and into my eyes.

It took us several minutes to regain our composure

and breath. Without a word, I started my car and drove on towards Mussoorie. None of us spoke until we reached the bus stand at Picture Palace.

'Your bravado would have gotten us killed,' Raman said sourly as he got off the car.

'Now do you believe that the *chudail* actually exists and the spot is haunted?'

'I am sorry. I really am,' I said and pressed the throttle.

It was well past 11.00 p.m. when I reached home. Without speaking to anyone I went to my room, locked the door and collapsed on the bed. I heard my mother calling me for dinner.

'I am not feeling well,' I shouted from my room.

That night I could not sleep a wink. I had a throbbing headache and took a paracetamol tablet, but that didn't help. I was in shock and kept trembling throughout the night. Whenever I closed my eyes, I could hear the wail and laughter of the chudail.

Next morning, I awoke with a high fever which persisted for a few days and I was forced to take leave from office.

I lost my appetite and did not feel like speaking to anyone. If someone spoke to me, I responded in monosyllables and gestures. My parents blamed this behaviour on my ill health. I hoped that the fever would continue for many more days so that I could continue to be on leave and avoid driving to Dehradun.

I did not speak about the incident to anyone at home, but over the next few days—based on the names disclosed by the constables—I called several acquaintances who had had encounters with this chudail.

'She asked me for a lift, sat on the back seat of my car and after a short distance I looked in the rear-view mirror and saw that there was no one. I was frightened out of my wits. I could have had a heart attack!' Ravi (name changed) said.

'I gave her a lift on my bike and when I tried to strike up a conversation she did not reply. I glanced back to find that she had simply disappeared. I got such a shock that I lost balance and crashed to the ground,' were the words of Samuel (name changed), a resident of Woodstock School.

I stayed practically locked up in my room for over 10 days, until finally my boss called and demanded that I rejoin office and attend to some urgent work.

'Oh God! What will happen? If I drive past that spot again, the chudail will haunt me for sure. Please protect me,' I earnestly prayed throughout the night.

Following the advice of friends, I kept a photo of Lord Hanuman in my car and reluctantly left for office the next morning.

While driving back from office in the evening, I raced past Chunakhala with the firm resolve to not stop the car for *any* woman asking for a lift.

'Even if she stands in the middle of the road, I will drive over her,' I decided.

My hands trembled as I held a lit cigarette—because I was told that ghosts do not come near fire—and kept

glancing fearfully in the rearview mirror in a bid to check that no unwanted passenger was sitting in the back seat of my car until I crossed the forsaken two kilometres stretch.

Thankfully the chudail did not make an appearance that evening or any of the subsequent evenings!

Meanwhile, Sudhir was back on active duty. I met him, Raman and Jogendra at Kolhukhet and we discussed the events of those two fateful nights.

'Nobody would believe us. We would become the laughing stock of the entire town and even worse, seen as cowards in our force,' Raman said.

'You are right,' said Jogendra. 'And we do not want to create unnecessary fear in the public mind,' he added.

So it was decided that none of us would tell anyone about the unusual events we had experienced.

But crossing Chunakhala continued to be a nightmare; driving swiftly—with a lit cigarette in hand and constant furtive glances in the rearview mirror to check for uninvited passengers—became a habitual routine.

Meanwhile, the town was gripped by fear as narratives of strange experiences at Chunakhala continued to spread. And like a Chinese whisper, they were distorted and exaggerated as they passed from person to person.

According to one story, a traveller passing through Chunakhala at night claimed to have seen lights dancing over the hills, with no source or explanation in sight. Over a dozen retellings, the lights had become will-o'-the-wisps.

'Through these lights the chudail is misguiding motorists to cause them to drive off the road into the gorge,' was the version of a certain gentleman as he solemnly narrated about the lights to several people in the town.

I wondered if the chudail had disclosed her plan to him.

Another story claimed that a woman from a nearby village was killed in a road accident while riding pillion on her husband's motorcycle, and *she* was the one who was asking for a lift.

'She hitchhikes so that she can reach her house every night to take care of her kids,' was what a friend said to me.

'But she is a spirit! Can't she just fly through the air and reach her house?' I enquired.

Each story, no matter how incredible, found eager listeners to excitedly absorb every detail. And with every retelling, the narratives expanded and grew more fantastical.

Time elapsed under the shadow of fear.

Sudhir got transferred to his hometown, Roorkee. 'I requested my seniors for a transfer. I feel unsafe here,' he said in our last conversation before he left Mussoorie for good. Next year Jogendra was transferred to Chamoli, but I never came to know about Raman's whereabouts.

While I continued to be tormented by the fear of this hitchhiking ghost, I could not stop wondering about the reason for this spirit to suddenly manifest itself.

'Hauntings on the Mussoorie-Dehradun road were never reported in the past. Why now?' I wondered.

The priest of a nearby temple used to visit our house frequently to examine the horoscopes of our family—my father was a firm believer.

One evening he came to meet father, who was not at home. As he sat on the sofa to wait for him, I sat alongside to keep him company.

Panditji must have been around 70 years of age. He was quite tall and had a slender frame. His long, flowing white beard cascaded below his neck, adding to his venerable appearance. He had a kind, cherubic demeanour and carried an aura of wisdom and kindness. Always adorned in a white kurta and dhoti, looking at him I was often reminded of Professor Dumbledore from the Harry Potter movies.

'Guruji, how can a place *suddenly* become haunted, where ghosts start to appear one fine day?' I asked him.

'Are you asking about Chunakhala, son?' he asked, a kind smile playing on his lips.

His answer caught me off guard. 'Yes, Guruji,' I blurted. 'How has Chunakhala, which was peaceful and normal for so long, suddenly become haunted?'

Panditji took a deep breath, leaned back, and gazed at the wooden ceiling of our house for a few seconds.

'Chunakhala may have become haunted due to several reasons—tragic events, unfinished business of the departed souls, or sudden disturbances in the spiritual energy of the area. Sometimes, it's a combination of all these factors.'

He paused, ensuring he had my full attention.

'Ghosts,' Panditji continued, 'are apparitions or manifestations of deceased individuals who could not leave the physical world after death.'

'According to Hindu mythology, it is believed that if proper last rites or funeral rituals are not performed for a deceased individual, their spirit may be unsettled or unable to find peace, and might haunt specific locations or objects,' he added.

'But why Chunakhala? It is in the middle of the forest with no settlement around, how can it be haunted?' I asked in one breath.

Panditji smiled understandingly. 'In order to understand why Chunakhala has become a hub of supernatural occurrences, it's essential to learn about the events at that place prior to the sighting of the apparition.'

I nodded, absorbing his wisdom. 'So, it's not just about the ghosts but about understanding the deeper stories and energies at play.'

Panditji nodded. 'But remember, son, not all spirits mean harm. Some may just be lost, seeking help to find their way. It's crucial to comprehend such situations rather than succumbing to fear,' he said.

'By the way, did you have an encounter with the ghost at Chunakhala?' He enquired with a mischievous smirk.

I was lost for words, not sure whether to reveal my ghastly experience to him. But by divine providence, my mother entered the room with tea and saved the day.

Later that night, alone in my room, I kept thinking

about what Panditji had said about souls unable to find peace and stuck in the physical world.

'He is such a learned man. I am sure whatever he is saying is correct,' I murmured.

But, as is often the case with the human mind, I got engrossed in my work and soon forgot about this discussion.

Several months later, following my customary routine, I headed towards Dehradun in the morning. The sun shone brightly in the spring sky and a gentle breeze rustled through the trees, carrying the refreshing fragrance of the forest.

'What a fine morning!' I murmured to myself.

But it turned out that my joy was short-lived.

As I reached Chunakhala, I saw a large crowd gathered by the road—at the exact spot where we had had that ghastly encounter with the ghost. There were a number of vehicles parked along the road.

As I slowed my car, I could also make out a large number of police personnel peering into the gorge from where we had heard the chudail's voice beckoning us!

My heart skipped a beat!

'Has the chudail finally inflicted harm upon someone?'

Overcome with panic, my first instinct was to drive past the spot. Yet somehow, I mustered the courage to stop. I stepped out of the car gingerly; I could feel my legs trembling and my heart pounding.

'What happened?' I asked a person standing at the

back of the crowd who was stretching himself on his tiptoes trying to peak over the others.

He glanced at me, his face white with fear and anxiety. 'There is a dead body,' he shouted amidst the clamour of voices.

'What?' I blurted; my voice was reduced to a whisper. I pushed forward, through the crowd, with a sense of dread. As I reached the front, a policeman stopped me with an outstretched hand.

'What's going on?' I asked.

'There is a body deep in the gorge; we are trying to recover it,' he explained with exasperation.

'Now get back,' he commanded sternly and gently pushed me back.

I was not keen on standing at that god-forsaken spot for much longer, and was getting late for work anyway, so I urgently pushed my way out of the crowd and drove on to Dehradun. But I found it difficult to drive along the winding hill road. The unsettling events weighed heavy on my mind.

There being no social media back in the day, I waited eagerly for next morning's newspaper. I woke up early and sprang to the door as soon as the soft rustling thud of its delivery sounded from the patio, eager to grab it before my father. Having claimed my prize, I swiftly retreated to the privacy of my room to read the news of the dead body found at Chunakhala the day before.

'Dead body of a woman found in a gorge at Chunakhala: Police suspect murder' was the headline.

The paper reported that some women from Bhatta had descended into the gorge to collect fodder leaves when one of them discovered a corpse. Terrified, they rushed back to their village and reported the matter to their families, who notified the police.

There was a statement from the police chief, who—based on the post-mortem report—confirmed that the corpse found in the gorge was of a middle-aged woman of about five feet in height; its decomposed state suggested that it had been there for several years. He further said that the skull of the victim had been crushed with a heavy object and that the police had registered a case of murder.

'After striking the woman on the head, the victim's body was apparently thrown down the gorge by the perpetrator,' the chief was quoted as saying.

After reading this news report, Panditji's words echoed in my mind.

'He was right!'

The chudail haunting Chunakhala was the disturbed spirit of this poor woman whose tragic end had left her soul unable to find peace.

I realized that this explained the sound we heard from the gorge that night. The woman's spirit was seeking help—trying to draw our attention to her body lying in the gorge.

'Perhaps her tormented soul would find peace now,' I muttered with a deep sigh, a sense of sorrow and empathy weighing down my words.

Once the woman's body was retrieved from the gorge, there were no more reports of commuters being accosted by her ghost.

The murderer of the poor woman was never found and the police closed the case after a few years; perhaps the removal of the body and a proper cremation of her remains acted as a form of closure for the tormented spirit.

Meanwhile, in my idyllic town—where people have a lot of time to bask leisurely under the warm sun, sipping tea—the hitchhiking ghost and her murder remained a hot topic of discussion for months. Such mysterious and haunting events provided ample fodder for conversations, stirring a mix of curiosity and speculation amongst the residents of Mussoorie.

But, dear reader, the story does not end here.

Several years' later, tragedy struck again in the form of an unfortunate and bizarre accident at Chunakhala. A Maruti car, coming from Jharipani, veered off the Chunakhala-Jharipani road and plummeted 500 feet down the slope to land on another vehicle on the Mussoorie-Dehradun road. The driver was alone in the Maruti but the car on which it landed had three passengers—two sitting on the front seat and a woman sitting in the back. The driver of the Maruti and the woman passenger of the other car were killed on the spot.

What was even more eerie and unsettling was the fact that the accident (where the car fell on top of another on Mussoorie-Dehradun road) occurred at the same spot where the motorists and my policeman friends claimed to have seen the chudail.

And as if this was not enough, this incident was followed by a number of accidents in the same vicinity. Incidents such as two-wheelers skidding on the road, collisions between vehicles, vehicles veering off the road, etc., were reported for almost a year.

'The chudail has returned!' A neighbour enthusiastically exclaimed as we sipped tea at his house.

'Are you looking forward to it? Perhaps you were eager to meet the charming chudail,' I teased, eliciting an angry glance from his wife.

That day, I learnt that the mere mention of another woman, even a chudail, can provoke jealousy and heartburn among wives!

Meanwhile, the residents were again gripped by fear and finally decided to take action.

The generally accepted belief, especially in the hills, is that constructing a small shrine or temple at places where ghosts have been sighted can help ward off evil spirits. Even places where accidents occur frequently are marked by small shrines on the roadside which, according to residents, help prevent further mishaps. I am sure that while travelling in the hills, you must have also come across such structures on the roadside—there are several such shrines on the Mussoorie-Dhanolti road.

So, to ward off the evil, the residents came together and decided to install an idol of Lord Hanuman at the place where the chudail was sighted in the past and where the accidents were occurring. Lo and behold! The temple did put an end to the accidents and everyone, including yours truly, breathed a sigh of relief.

But so many questions remain unanswered.

Who was the woman whose dead body was found? Who murdered her and why? Was it her spirit that was seen on the road? Has the spirit found peace? Why did that strange accident occur even after the dead body of the woman was removed? Are the spirits of the victims of that accident also wandering there? Has the temple been able to contain the spirits?

Let me end this story with another personal anecdote.

In the winter of 2016, I was returning alone from Dehradun. It must have been 10.00 p.m. when my car malfunctioned and stopped—guess what—at the exact same spot where the chudail was seen and the accidents had happened.

I was terrified!

'This time the chudail will surely kill me,' I thought as my teeth clattered while I loudly chanted Hanuman Chalisa.

Thankfully, I was rescued by a taxi driver who was driving down from Mussoorie. He helped me fix the malfunction and saved my soul, leaving me alive to write this story for you!

Maybe the spirit of the woman is still lurking around at Chunakhala; maybe it has found two companions in the form of the victims of the road accident; maybe there will be more eerie incidents...

Your guess is as good as mine!

# The Cursed Cottage

The Mountain Lodge was constructed in the mid-nineteenth century by a British army officer—Colonel Macmillan—as his summer abode. Located a few kilometres ahead of Woodstock School, nestled amidst dense deodar forests, this splendid house provided breathtaking views of the Doon valley.

One reached Mountain Lodge by navigating either treacherous trails on horseback—along narrow roads hugging steep cliffs—or a strenuous five kilometres uphill trek from the Mall Road. But the scenic beauty, enchanting vistas and solitude of the place made the effort worth its while.

The approach from the main road to the building was a bridle path carved out of the hill. Majestic deodar trees stood guard on both sides, creating a verdant canopy that led visitors to the lodge.

Apparently, the colonel had built two cottages in his estate. The first one was located on an adjoining ridge and was made for his brother, while the much grander Mountain Lodge was meant for himself.

The colonel capitalized on the abundant deodar trees in his estate and generated substantial income from their sale. He also obtained valuable timber for the construction of the houses.

However, his stay at Mountain Lodge was short-lived. After a few decades, he sold the house and moved out of Mussoorie. Sources indicate that Macmillan was transferred to South India and he purchased a house in Ooty.

The lodge remained vacant for a while until it was rented to a philanthropic society for establishing a school. But the remote location, problems of water supply and a fire forced the school management to relocate. Thus, Mountain Lodge was abandoned again and remained unoccupied for several years, until another English gentleman took ownership of the property around 1910. It continued to change hands until a Mr Sharma from Mumbai purchased it in 1992.

By then, the 'grand' Mountain Lodge had become a crumbling, dilapidated structure that had remained unoccupied for several decades. No one in town could recall its original name any more and the house was more popularly known as the 'haunted house'.

It was believed that Mountain Lodge was the centre of paranormal activity where inexplicable and eerie happenings had been reported for decades. Townsfolk spoke of it in hushed tones and over the years tales spun like spider silk—about restless spirits that clung to the house, phantom footsteps on creaking floorboards, spectral figures that people claimed to have seen through its mist-shrouded windows, and mournful wails that pierced moonless nights.

Mr Sharma acquired the house at a throwaway price since the previous owner was apparently desperate to get rid of the property. The dubious reputation of the house was indeed a dampener, but considering the price, Mr Sharma was willing to take the risk.

However, he found it difficult to hire a chowkidar for Mountain Lodge as no one was willing to stay in the house. Everyone shook their head, eyes wide with fear. 'No one stays there,' they murmured.

Kirat Singh was a native of a village in Tehri Garhwal. About 40 years old, he had a medium height but an extremely slim build. Kirat Singh had a fair complexion with a small and round face etched with numerous wrinkles—a testimony to the hardships endured over the years. This harsh exterior was offset by his soft voice and pleasant manners. Kirat used to work as a chowkidar in an estate near Lal Tibba for many years, but lost his job when the estate was sold to new owners. Desperate for employment, he quickly agreed to work as a chowkidar for Mr Sharma.

His friends and relatives working in Mussoorie, and even chowkidars from neighbouring houses, all warned him to stay away from Mountain Lodge. Their eyes held fear and their voices were hushed. 'Stay away,' everyone pleaded. 'Evil resides in the house; there have been unexplained accidents and even death of earlier occupants.'

Defying everyone, Kirat declared that he was no stranger to hardships. He had faced hunger, storms and the biting cold of winters.

'Ghosts don't scare me,' he scoffed. 'I've faced worse.'

He grabbed the keys of the house from Mr Sharma and set out for the 'haunted' mansion. As he approached the house, the howling of the wind intensified, playing a mournful symphony; the deodar trees that stood sentinel around the house swayed in unison, issuing a silent warning.

Mountain Lodge was a one-storey house with a rusty tin roof and a long porch at the entrance. There were remnants of a flower bed at the boundary of the porch but the flowers had vanished long ago. The walls—last painted decades ago—had plaster peeling off at many places, revealing brick and stone masonry. The wooden windows stood bare, most of their panes missing and lost to time.

Showing a hint of nerves, Kirat opened the door of the house, which grunted loudly as if reluctant to admit him. The air hung heavy, laden with the scent of damp and decay. The uneven wooden planks of the floor creaked underfoot, as if groaning in pain. Sunlight filtered through the windows and cast elongated shadows upon the floorboards.

Furniture, long abandoned and decaying, stood like silent witnesses to forgotten memories. A cracked mirror reflected fractured images. The fireplace, once a source of warmth and comfort, now harboured cold ashes and the memories of long-extinguished flames.

After a look around, Kirat decided to tend to the house to make it liveable. He swept away cobwebs, cleaned the floors and dusted the paltry furniture that remained usable.

As the sun dipped below the horizon, he lit the oil lamps he had bought from the market. Their warm glow pushed back the encroaching darkness. Tired after the cleaning drive, Kirat had the few rotis and vegetables he had brought from the market for dinner. As night approached, he fell into a deep slumber on a rickety bed in one corner of the bedroom. Next morning, he fetched water from a spring below the house and stacked firewood gathered from the surrounding forest.

Days passed and Kirat settled comfortably in his new dwelling. Apart from the occasional howling of the wind, rustling of trees, distant growls of leopards and melodious chirping of birds, no untoward sound disturbed his peace of mind.

'People were unnecessarily making up stories about the house,' he thought.

One evening, as dusk settled in, Kirat made his way back to the house with provisions in hand, walking briskly along the bridle path that led to the house from the main road.

'It's getting late,' he murmured, 'and I still need to cook my dinner.'

Just then, as if conjured by twilight itself, he saw the figure of a woman standing silhouetted against the fading light. Startled at first, Kirat assumed that she must be a resident of a nearby village.

As he came closer, the woman glanced at him. She

had large black eyes, framed by long lashes and flowing hair. Her skin was fair and unblemished, her nose was small and delicate, and her lips were full and well-shaped. She was dressed in traditional Garhwali attire comprising a red coloured ghagra (a long, flared skirt), a black choli (a waist length, full-sleeved blouse), and a red dupatta*.

Kirat couldn't help but murmur, 'God! She is beautiful.'

In that fleeting moment, as if able to read Kirat's thoughts, the woman's lips curled into a teasing smile. Unaccustomed to such attention from women, he stood dumbfounded, heart racing like a startled deer.

Without uttering a single word, the woman moved swiftly and veered off the bridle path, following a narrow goat trail into the forest. Kirat remained rooted to the ground, his gaze tracing the woman's silhouette until she vanished out of sight.

He was struck by cupid! He kept thinking about the woman and saw her in his dreams, standing before him and smiling.

Desperation gnawed at Kirat's heart. Yearning to meet the woman again, he spent every evening waiting at the spot where he had seen her. He stood there until the sun dipped below the horizon—patient, hopeful, and a touch foolish—and even went down the goat path the

---

*As per traditional attire of Garhwal, the women wrap the dupatta around their shoulders and then tie it across their waist.

woman had taken, only to realize that it led deeper into the forest.

Finally, losing all hopes of meeting her again, Kirat gave up his vigil.

'Who was she? Was she for real or was I imagining things?' He kept wondering.

Weeks later, Kirat sat upon the weathered porch of the house, leisurely sipping a cup of tea. The setting sun cast a warm golden hue across the landscape.

He casually glanced towards the bridle path and the sight that caught his eyes made the cup slip from his trembling hands—staining his shirt with spilled tea—as he gasped in disbelief. There, at the precise spot where he had first met her, stood the 'mysterious woman' with her back turned towards Kirat.

'Hey! Hey lady, STOP!' He shouted at the top of his voice, fearful that the woman might disappear down the goat path again.

The woman, her silhouette framed by the fading light, pivoted slowly in Kirat's direction and smiled as she saw him running towards her at full speed.

Panting and puffing, Kirat reached the woman. 'Where were you all these days?' He blurted. 'I was waiting for you.'

'And why would you wait for me?' She asked with a teasing smile. Her soft melodious voice seemed to echo through the forest.

Kirat stood there, caught between awe and nervousness.

'I…uh… I wanted to meet you again,' he stammered.

'You've managed to do that,' she laughed. 'Now I must go.'

With graceful steps, she descended towards the goat path—the same trail by which she had disappeared the other day.

'Wait,' Kirat shouted. 'When will you meet again?'

'Tomorrow,' she said after a deliberate pause, and ran down the trail.

The next day Kirat did not feel like doing any work—he did not even cook his food and ate the leftovers—and waited eagerly on the porch.

Exactly at dusk, the woman made her appearance.

Kirat stepped towards her, heart racing.

'Hello, I am Kirat Singh,' he introduced himself. 'What is your name?'

'Gori,' she replied.

'Where do you live?' Kirat enquired.

'I live down below,' Gori replied cryptically, her gaze drifting towards the shadowed depths of the forest.

Kirat figured that she was from the village down in the valley below the house.

'I live in this house,' Kirat pointed to the weathered building behind him.

'I know,' Gori chuckled. 'Now I have to go,' she said and turned to leave.

Kirat desperately begged her to stay, until Gori promised to return the following day. And so she did— the next day, the day after, and the day after that.

Their meetings became a ritual—just as dusk painted the sky, she would appear at the same spot while Kirat stood outside his house, waiting. They would have a short conversation and then Gori would leave.

Kirat told her almost everything about himself. But he deliberately concealed the fact that he had a wife—who toiled in the fields back in his village—and a teenage son. He noticed that Gori did not open up and was reluctant to speak about herself.

'Let's talk about something else,' she would say, her eyes distant. 'Tell me more about Lal Tibba,' she would ask, with curiosity that seemed genuine. 'And Mussoorie market—I've never been there. What is it like?'

Meanwhile, Kirat had fallen head over heels in love with Gori. Her company made him forget about his wife and son. Thoughts of a life with Gori bloomed like wildflowers in his mind.

'I can marry her,' Kirat mused, his conscience tiptoeing on the edge of betrayal. 'My wife will never know.'

He awaited an opportunity to convey his feelings to Gori.

One evening, as Gori returned along the narrow trail, Kirat followed her. She implored him to go away but Kirat kept following until they reached a small clearing in the forest.

Gori settled on a large rock that bordered the clearing.

'So you won't go away?' She was angry and exasperated.

'I will accompany you to your village,' Kirat replied.

Gori signalled him to sit beside her. 'Kirat, promise me that you will never follow me. I do not want my family to know about you.'

Reluctantly, Kirat made the promise, though his heart rebelled against it.

'But Gori, I am in love with you. I want to spend more time with you,' he confessed, emboldened by the invitation to sit beside her.

He reached for her hand with trembling fingers, but Gori withdrew her hand with surprising swiftness and moved away.

'What happened?' He asked sheepishly.

'Kirat, you must behave yourself,' Gori snapped, her nostrils flaring with anger and her face contorting with fury.

'Now go away,' her words sliced through the air. 'I don't want to see you again.'

Kirat was scared of losing Gori. He sank to his knees. 'Please,' he implored, 'calm down. This will never happen again.'

There followed a long silence, until Kirat sensed that Gori had calmed down. Still on his knees, Kirat gathered courage and asked, 'Will you come and live in the house with me?'

The sun had set by now and darkness enveloped the clearing.

Gori seemed to have been waiting for this invitation. For a fleeting moment her lips curled into an evil grin;

her black eyes turned crimson and her flawless skin developed the deep wrinkles that come with age.

Despite the darkness, Kirat felt the change in Gori. But before he could utter a word, Gori had regained her normal countenance, looking as desirable as ever.

'If I come to live with you,' Gori enquired, 'will you allow me complete freedom to do as I please?'

'Of course.'

'You need to swear upon God. Repeat after me, "God, I am allowing Gori to live in my house and giving her complete freedom to do as she pleases."'

Kirat found this quite amusing. He repeated Gori's words and laughed; his laughter echoed through the night.

Gori smiled.

'Very well, Kirat,' she said. 'You return to the house. I shall be there shortly.'

Like an obedient child, Kirat turned and walked back to the house. Moonlight filtered through the trees and the large deodars cast long, eerie shadows across the narrow path. The wind wailed mournfully while a distant howling of wolves filled the air, as if warning of some impending danger.

Lost in his thoughts, Kirat remained oblivious to these omens. His heart thumped with excitement as he looked forward to the arrival of Gori.

Upon reaching the house, he lit the oil lamps and got busy preparing dinner.

'I think I will cook for two as Gori will be joining me tonight,' he thought and quickly put the vegetables to boil and kneaded the special *mandua* (finger millet) flour that he had received from home.

That is when he heard it—the soft tread of footsteps.

'Gori has come!' He exclaimed and opened the door. Apart from the moonlight spilling in, there was no one there.

Again, he heard the soft tread of footsteps. This time, the floorboards creaked behind him.

Bewildered, Kirat swivelled around and found Gori standing inside the room. Her face was an ethereal blend of beauty and malevolence. Her pale, unblemished skin was almost luminescent now, emitting a soft, ghostly glow. Her dark eyes, once alluring, were blood-red and seemed to pierce through Kirat's soul. Long, dark lashes framed those haunting eyes. Her picture-perfect lips were contorted into a cruel smile—the corners of her mouth curving sinisterly upwards—revealing teeth that gleamed menacingly in the dim light.

The breeze swept through the open door and stirred her long black hair, adding to her otherworldly aura.

'Who...who are you?' He stammered, barely audible.

'I am Gori, your love...' was the reply.

'No, you are not Gori. Get out of this house immediately,' Kirat's voice was a mere croak.

'I will not go now. You have sworn to God to allow me into this house!' Gori laughed menacingly.

Kirat's trembling hands gripped the doorframe as he wondered if he had unwittingly invited a malevolent force into his home. A cold dread gripped his heart.

He realized that Gori was no mortal woman but a ghost—an evil spirit!

Kirat's fear was palpable. His hands had become numb and his feet were paralyzed—he wanted to run but could not move—his breaths came in shallow gasps, and every nerve in his body was screaming.

The room seemed to be closing in.

'Yes. I am not mortal,' Gori said, as if reading Kirat's mind.

'I am the ghost of Gori, whose head was once brutally crushed here by her husband. My soul has been seeking revenge for a very long time,' she hissed. 'Many years ago, I was forced to leave this house. But now you have unwittingly invited me back.'

Her eyes gleamed with otherworldly malice as her demonic laughter pierced the air. 'Now, I will exact my vengeance upon every man who dares enter this house!'

Gori's menacing advance set Kirat's heart racing. As beads of sweat formed on his forehead and his body trembled, he became sure that these were his final moments. Gori's vengeful spirit would show no mercy.

He braced himself for the inevitable.

As Gori's outstretched hands drew near, Kirat winced in fear and swayed backwards in his desperation to evade her. In the process, his grip on the decaying doorframe weakened and he tumbled backward, crashing out of the door into the moonlit night.

Gori's ghostly form appeared in the doorway, her face twisted in anger and eyes aflame with wrath. She stood there, shouting in frustration, as Kirat lay sprawled on the ground, gasping for breath. Perhaps the doorway acted as a barrier—one that Gori could not cross, once inside.

Kirat quickly scrambled to his feet and ran like a madman along the bridle pathway. Fear gnawed at him as he glanced back, checking if Gori was pursuing him. But she remained framed in the doorway.

Kirat ran towards the nearby market—desperation and fear fuelling his sprint—and collapsed outside the provision shop. Sundru the shopkeeper, who slept inside the shop, opened the shutter to investigate the commotion. His eyes widened in surprise as he found Kirat lying unconscious on the road.

It was midday when Kirat came to his senses. Gori's ghostly presence still haunted him and his heart raced as he fearfully glanced around the room to ensure that she was not around.

After he made sure that Gori's vengeful spirit had not followed him, Kirat narrated the night's ordeal to Sundru.

'I always heard that the old house was haunted,' Sundru mused. 'It seems that you had a lucky escape.'

He was concerned that Gori's ghost might still continue to haunt Kirat.

'I've heard that some ghosts can travel from place to place. What if she follows you and causes harm?' Sundru pondered with his brows knitted together. The thought sent a shiver down Kirat's spine. Could Gori's wrath stretch beyond the Lodge's threshold?

Sundru advised him to go to the old *tantrik baba* who lived at Mullingar.

'Baba has powers to deal with *bhoot, pret,* chudail and all kinds of evil. I strongly advise you to meet him.'

Kirat immediately set off to meet the baba.

He crossed Mullingar building and turned left, according to Sundru's directions, to follow a path that ran below it. After walking a bit further, he turned right onto a narrow trail that branched off the main path.

Kirat felt nervous as he tread on the trail to the baba's house. 'Will baba be able to contain the evil of Gori?' He wondered as he increased his pace in an effort to outrun his doubts. The trail culminated at an unassuming two-storey building. The ground floor was divided into four rooms—two flanking each side.

Kirat's gaze fixed upon the first room to the right, with a metal trident adorning the lintel above the door—poised to ward off evil. Drawn upon the door was the sacred symbol of *Om*, whose curves and angles held the resonance of ancient chants.

Kirat's heart raced; he was sure that this was the dwelling of the baba! With trembling hands, he gently knocked on the door.

The door was opened by a tall man wearing a long kurta and dhoti. His sun-kissed skin had a rich, earthy complexion and his face was etched with deep lines that drew the map of a well-lived life.

His long, unkempt silver hair brushed against his shoulders while his matching silver beard, thick and tangled, extended to his chest, couched in a garland of hundreds of *rudraksh* beads. His wide forehead bore a broad layer of ash with a sandalwood *tilak* at its centre signifying the auspicious third *netra*. But the man's most striking features were his eyes. Deep and wise, they seemed to peer beyond Kirat's physical form into the very tapestry of his soul. He could sense an aura of otherworldly power emanating from him.

'Namaskar, Baba ji,' he greeted with reverence, his hands folded.

Baba ji returned his greeting with a smile that creased his weathered face with gentle lines.

'Come inside, son...' he beckoned.

As Kirat stepped into the small room where Baba lived, a strong smell of incense hit his nostrils. To the left, a narrow passage led to a modest kitchen and a toilet, while on the right stood a large statue of the goddess Kali surrounded by smaller framed pictures of other deities on the wall behind her. Kirat felt their gazes follow him.

A human skull was kept in front of the idol and its presence was unsettling. Its jaw, agape in a perpetual grin, seemed to mock Kirat, while its gaze—empty yet all-seeing—stared curiously at him. 'Is this real? Or merely a macabre ornament,' Kirat wondered.

In front of the idol, a mat was placed on the ground and on one side of the mat was a cushion indicating the seat of the Baba. A copper plate beside the cushion held a small copper pot (*lota*) filled with water, a small silver trident and a tiny bowl containing sandalwood paste.

Behind it was an open cupboard, haphazardly stacked with numerous old books and manuscripts that seemed as old as eternity. Kirat imagined that they were filled with spells, prophecies and forgotten hymns used by the Baba to control evil.

Baba took his seat on the cushion and motioned Kirat to sit on the mat. 'The skull is real but it will not harm you,' he reassured him, sensing Kirat's hesitation. 'So what brings you here, my son?'

Kirat began hesitantly, 'Baba ji, I work as the chowkidar at Mountain Lodge...'

Before he could finish, the baba interjected with a hint of amusement, 'Ah, so you're the "mad chowkidar"?'

'Mad chowkidar?' Kirat echoed, perplexed.

'Yes,' Baba replied with a glint in his eyes. 'Everyone calls you that ever since you took up the job at Mountain Lodge.'

Kirat explained that despite repeated warnings, his desperation for employment drove him to accept the chowkidar's position.

And then, with a storyteller's urgency, Kirat narrated what had transpired with him since he started working there—he recounted his meetings with Gori, how she gained entry into the house on that fateful night, and attempted to take his life.

'You actually pledged to God that Gori could live in the house?' Baba exclaimed. 'A *grave* mistake!'

'I am sorry Baba, I was enamoured by her beauty.'

Baba's eyes held both understanding and gravity.

'Gori possesses a cunning charm,' he acknowledged. 'She ensnares men with her beauty.'

Kirat's incredulity spilled forth. 'Baba ji, do you know Gori personally?'

Baba leaned back, his gaze distant. 'Yes,' he replied, 'I encountered Gori when I was a young man—maybe 56 years ago.'

'What happened, Baba?'

With a deep sigh, Baba recollected the events that transpired over half a century ago.

After learning *tantra vidhya* from his guru on the ghats of Benaras, he decided to return to the hills and help the people of the mountains.

Baba's eyes, like polished stones, met Kirat's.

'I walked these hills, going from village to village. The people—simple and superstitious—welcomed me. I not only rid them of malevolent spirits but also performed rituals to prevent crop failures and illnesses.'

'And what about Gori?' Kirat asked impatiently.

Baba smiled. 'Yes. I am coming to that, my son.'

In the 1930s, the Mountain Lodge was bought by a wealthy Indian businessman as his summer abode. As the family settled, the house stirred.

Baba stared at the ceiling and seemed lost in thought. He recalled the events—the creaking floors, flickering lamps, shadows dancing across moonlit corridors, footsteps echoing when no one was around, doors swinging open unbidden, voices murmuring in empty rooms. The family was distressed.

'One night, the owner felt as if someone was choking him. He opened his eyes in panic and gazed into the cruel face of a woman whose hands were clasped around his neck,' Baba said.

'Was that Gori?' Kirat asked, to which Baba nodded in affirmation.

The man struggled to break free but the grip was unyielding. Thankfully, his wife—sleeping next to him—woke up and shrieked, which made the spectre disappear. The scared owner sent his family packing and approached Baba for help.

'I went to the house with the owner and I started a puja to dispel the evil. It took me several hours to control and bind the evil spirit, making her appear before me. "Why are you haunting this house?" I asked, and forced the malevolent spirit to narrate her tale.'

Baba then narrated Gori's story:

*She and her husband Ramu were natives of a village in Uttarkashi. More than a hundred years ago, they came here in search of work and found employment in a brick-kiln owned by an Englishman.*

*Ramu was of a dark complexion and had average features, in stark contrast to Gori's radiant beauty. While Ramu was proud of his beautiful wife, each glance from other men etched doubts into his mind.*

*The Englishman—the kiln's owner—frequently came to the kiln. His seemingly innocuous visits ignited Ramu's suspicions. One day—returning after transporting bricks to a construction site—he saw the Englishman speaking to Gori at the kiln. Both of them were laughing loudly.*

*Ramu was furious with rage. After the Englishman left, he accused Gori of having an affair with him. When she denied, Ramu pushed her to the ground and crushed her skull with a brick.*

*He dragged the body to the clearing in the forest, located on the goat path, and buried her there. But he realized the grave nature of this deed and ran away to his village.*

*The Englishman suspected foul play and notified the police, and Ramu was captured. He quickly confessed to his crime and was hanged in Dehradun.*

*Since her murder, Gori had been wandering at the kiln, seeking revenge from every man and even killed two people who had come to work there. A few years later, the Englishman decided to demolish the kiln and build a house at the site. Thus, Mountain Lodge sprang from the ashes of the kiln. But Gori continued to haunt the place, looking for revenge.*

Baba said that he chanted some mantras in a bid to end Gori's existence but was unable to do so.

'She had a deep-rooted hatred which made her evil too powerful. I only managed to get her out of the house and bind her at the place where she was buried.'

'Then how did she come inside the house, Baba?' Kirat asked.

'Because of *your* foolishness,' Baba roared. 'Bound by my spell, she could never have entered the house. But you allowed her inside.'

Kirat's cheeks flushed crimson with shame. 'Baba ji, please help me! Protect me from Gori,' he cried.

Baba placed a hand on Kirat's shoulder. 'Don't worry, my son.'

Kirat, still flushed with shame and fear, found solace in this promise of protection.

'Kirat, I will prepare for the rituals. Day after tomorrow, we venture to the haunted house to put an end to Gori's unholy existence,' Baba declared solemnly.

It was late evening when the duo reached Mountain Lodge on the designated day. Kirat entered the house crouching behind Baba like a shadow and peered into the dark room. Baba admonished him and asked him to come forth and light a lamp.

'No harm will come to you as long as I am here,' he promised.

Baba took out turmeric powder from the cloth bag that hung from his shoulder and made a cross on the floor while chanting some mantras, before sitting down on it. He did the same on the floor to his left and asked Kirat to sit upon it.

'Whatever happens, do not get up,' Baba warned.

Next, he retrieved a skull from his bag and set it on the floor and carefully drew a large circle of *roli* around it. Then, he took out the copper plate, the lota and the silver trident, and arranged them within the circle. He filled the lota with *Gangajal*, lit a diya within the circle and placed some incense sticks nearby. Their fragrant smoke curled into the air.

As the sun dipped below the horizon, casting long shadows through the timeworn windows, Baba began his sacred ritual. As his voice rose to a crescendo, reverberating across the house, Baba's countenance changed. His face looked cruel and menacing, and his eyes glowed liked embers. He grasped the silver trident and swung it in a sweeping arc, as if cleaving through the very fabric of evil.

Kirat watched in awe.

Suddenly, the sound of demonic laughter emanated from inside the house. Kirat wanted to run away but Baba's presence reassured him.

A strong wind started blowing, threatening to blow away everything in its path, but Baba's spell—an invisible shield—held firm, and not a feather stirred, not a leaf trembled.

Soon, the loud laughter turned into desperate wails. The house itself seemed to protest—floorboards groaned, windows rattled, window panes crashed and furniture turned upside down. Gori tried to break Baba's concentration but he held his ground with the tenacity of a banyan tree.

Finally, after several hours, the evil's grip loosened. Its fury waned and the gusts of wind and the rattling of windows stopped. Gori was forced to appear before them—her eyes pools of sorrow and rage, her face contorted in fury.

Baba took out a bottle from his bag and attempted to capture the spirit, but as before, the evil and hate was too strong to be confined. Laughing loudly, Gori flew out of the door.

'Where is she going?' Kirat shrieked in despair and fear.

'She is going to the clearing where her body is buried. Now she can never enter the house and she will be powerless to cause any harm outside it,' Baba assured him.

Thus ended the haunting of Mountain Lodge!

Kirat wanted to quit his work, but Baba stopped him.

'Why do you want to quit a good job? Gori is gone; she is powerless now.'

He handed a *tabiz* to Kirat and asked him to wear it around his neck.

'This will protect you, my son.'

With Baba's reassurance, Kirat continued with his job and never encountered Gori again.

Sometime later, while still working as a chowkidar at Mountain Lodge, Kirat came to work for my father in his office. He worked for him during the day and performed his duties at the Lodge from evening onwards. He shared his story with my father. Intrigued by the tale, my father recounted it to me, sparking my curiosity in turn. I persuaded Kirat to tell me the story again and he repeated it in intricate detail, like an experienced storyteller.

A few years hence, Kirat quit his job at my father's office citing ill health. However, he still visited us occasionally, bringing wild berries and fruits from the forest around Mountain Lodge.

One day, my father told me that Kirat was no more.

'What happened?' I asked.

'He was found in the house with his skull crashed in. Police suspect murder,' father said sadly. Apparently, the police apprehended the chowkidar of a nearby house but released him due to lack of evidence.

'Skull crashed...'

It made me wonder.

Was it the handiwork of Gori? Had her spirit managed to enter the house again? Did she exact revenge upon Kirat? Was the tabiz not able to protect him?

Anyway, Mountain Lodge was demolished a few years ago and replaced by a multi-storeyed building.

Does Gori haunt the new occupants of the house?

Only time will tell.

# The Silent Sentinel

It was past midnight. A dense monsoon fog enveloped the air, as Narri and Sanju huddled behind the rusting gate of Harding Cottage and stared outside.

A few paces behind them, perched on his haunches, was Sobhanu—the steadfast chowkidar of the cottage—his eyes squinting as if trying to peer through the mist. Bhura, his loyal Bhutia dog, sat sentinel alongside, his ears pricked and nostrils flaring.

Behind them stood the imposing Harding Cottage, its timeworn facade obscured by tendrils of fog. Its windows—barely visible—seemed to hold secrets within.

And so they waited—a motley crew of sentries bound by curiosity and racing heartbeats!

The ever-impulsive Sanju leaned towards Sobhanu and whispered, 'Will he appear tonight, *chacha*?' Narri shot him a reproachful look and motioned him to be quiet.

At that moment, Bhura—who could sense more than any human—became restless. He looked at Sobhanu with pleading eyes, imploring his master to retire to the sanctuary of the cottage. A low warning growl rumbled from his mouth.

And then he appeared: a tall, stockily built man, whose broad shoulders and sturdy frame gave him an imposing appearance. He wore a dark robe and a bowler hat, whose brim cast a shadow over his features. His long and pointed face was obscured by a thick beard. His eyes, although hidden beneath the hat, glinted with an otherworldly light.

The man's footsteps had no sound as he seemed to glide effortlessly through the air. He did not glance at the onlookers but carried straight ahead, past the gate, along the narrow road that led to the main bazaar.

Sanju's heart skipped a beat while Narri—wide-eyed and trembling—instinctively drew back from the gate. Even Bhura lowered his head and tucked his tail between his legs. But Sobhanu's gaze didn't waver. Perhaps he had encountered this enigmatic figure countless times during his nightly vigils.

It was several minutes before Sanju could whisper, 'Chacha, was this the ghost you were talking about?'

Sobhanu nodded.

'Yes son, I encounter this ghost almost every night during my rounds of the cottage. He passes just outside the gate, his eyes fixed on the road, as he glides through the air towards Gandhi Chowk.'

Sobhanu had recently been appointed the chowkidar of this cottage after the previous person was removed following several burglaries. Ever since, the spectre of the tall man in a dark robe had become a fixture of Sobhanu's nocturnal vigil.

Initially—not realizing that it was a ghost—Sobhanu wondered why a living soul would venture out at such late hours. He even called out to it once, but was not acknowledged. Days later, when clarity dawned—that the figure was not a mortal but a spectral presence with an inexplicable nightly ritual—terror had gripped Sobhanu. He was afraid of its potential intrusion through the cottage gate.

'What if it harms me?' He had shuddered.

So he stopped venturing close to the iron gate and instead kept vigil from the verandah of the cottage. He even stopped blowing his whistle around the time of the phantom's arrival.

He sought reassurance from local residents, who confirmed the ghost's long-standing presence in the neighbourhood. But they also assured him that the spectral figure had never harmed anyone, which helped dispel his fear.

Meanwhile, Sobhanu's nephew Sanju and his friend Narri had left their village in pursuit of employment. The young men, both in their early twenties, had found temporary refuge with Sobhanu. Their mischievous and free-spirited nature often clashed with their uncle's more reserved temperament.

Inadvertently, one day they overheard Sobhanu speaking to his friend about the spectre. The very mention of a ghost ignited their adventurous spirits and Sobhanu was forced to eventually acquiesce to their demand to show them the ghost.

However, seeing the apparition only further ignited their curiosity.

'Chacha, where does this ghost go?' Sanju asked the next morning.

'I do not know, son,' Sobhanu replied as he leaned back in his creaky chair, the morning sun casting shadows on the floor of his one-room house located behind Harding Cottage. 'Some claim to have glimpsed him near the bazaar. But beyond that, his path remains a mystery.'

'We've got to find out where he goes,' Narri declared, his eyes sparkling with anticipation. Sanju nodded enthusiastically, eager for the adventure.

Sobhanu shook his head.

'No boys, it's not wise. We don't know what he is or why he's here. It's best to leave him alone.'

But the seed of intrigue had been planted. Ignoring their uncle's warnings, the young men returned to their post behind the rusting iron gate the next night. The fog wrapped around them like a spectral curtain.

As midnight approached, the ghostly figure reappeared, gliding past the Harding Cottage gate towards the bazaar. With heart pounding, Sanju cautiously opened the creaking gate. '*Shh...*' Narri hissed, his eyes wide with fear and excitement.

The phantom, however, continued uphill, undeterred by the noise and seemingly oblivious of their presence.

The duo followed him cautiously, keeping a safe distance as they tiptoed through the night, their breath held in anticipation.

The figure went past the bazaar, effortlessly ascending the steep incline. Sanju and Narri struggled to keep up, their breaths coming in ragged gasps.

'Where is he going?' Sanju huffed.

'I can't keep up,' Narri panted, 'let's go back.' But a determined Sanju urged him on.

Finally, they reached the imposing gates of a boarding school. The heavy iron gates were firmly shut, but the spectral figure passed effortlessly through and vanished into the night.

'Did you see that?' Narri's voice trembled. Both the young men were fearful now.

'Why did he come to the school?' Sanju wondered.

In the following days, they met a few of Sobhanu's friends who shared more information about the mysterious figure. 'This ghost has never harmed anyone, never looked at anyone—he just follows his path,' Bhola assured them. 'It seems he is a noble soul, unable to move on to the other world.'

Sanju and Narri kept wondering about the ghost. Not satisfied with finding its route, the two mischief-mongers concocted new plans.

'Narri, everyone says the ghost does not pay attention to anyone. Let's find out for sure,' Sanju suggested, his eyes gleaming.

'But how?' Narri asked, his curiosity piqued.

Sanju leaned in and shared his plan in hushed tones. As the details unfolded, Narri's face lit up with excitement.

'This will be fun!' Narri exclaimed, nodding gleefully. 'But what if the ghost gets angry and harms us?' He enquired cautiously.

'You heard what they said. This ghost is a noble soul. He has never harmed anyone.'

Satisfied, the young pranksters planned their next move and went to the market to buy the items required for their plan. The following night, as the ghostly figure passed Harding Cottage, Sanju and Narri followed closely, their hearts pounding with anticipation. A short distance ahead, they halted and took out some firecrackers from their pockets, ignited them and hurled them at the spectre. A series of loud explosions echoed through the night.

The ghostly figure continued on its upward journey, undisturbed.

'He didn't even react!' Narri exclaimed in astonishment.

Sanju nodded, his brow furrowed in thought. 'I have another idea,' he declared with a cunning smile.

They spent the next couple of days planning and preparing. 'This is a bit dangerous. I feel scared,' Narri protested. But Sanju reassured him with a confident smile.

With their preparations complete, the two young men ventured out of the house a little before midnight. Walking a short distance uphill, they reached a narrow bridle path that branched off to the right of the main road and ascended into the darkness. Sanju and Narri walked up the steep path until they reached their vantage point a few feet above the main road.

There, they sat waiting...

Soon their target appeared, gliding through the air. As he passed below them, Sanju and Narri picked up the stones they had piled by the bridle path the previous day—and started hurling them at the apparition. To their astonishment, they passed straight through the apparition without causing any disturbance, and clattered loudly on the road, echoing through the night. The ghost continued its ethereal journey, completely unaffected.

'Throw more stones,' Sanju directed and both of them rained down a barrage of stones.

It was as if they had tested the patience of the ghost.

Suddenly, the figure stopped and turned his face in the direction from where the stones were being pelted. Sanju and Narri froze, their laughter replaced by cold dread.

The man's eyes, burning like crimson embers, locked onto them. With a menacing gesture, he raised his right hand, clenched his fist and made a downward motion, as if pulling an invisible rope. An unseen force seized Sanju and Narri, lifted them off their feet and tossed them violently on the road below, directly in the way of the spectral figure.

The prankster duo lay sprawled on the cold, hard road for hours, crying in pain and trembling with fear, unable to get up.

Finally, as dawn approached, a passer-by stumbled upon the injured boys. Alarms were raised, and soon a group of concerned locals, including Sobhanu and his friends, arrived at the scene. Two strong porters were summoned to carry the injured men to the Landour Community Hospital.

Sanju had fractures in both legs and bruises on his hands and chest; Narri had fractures in one hand and one leg, and was missing two front teeth, not to speak of the bruises all over his body.

They stayed in the hospital for over a week, being cared for by their uncle and his friends. However, they were extremely traumatized and hardly spoke or ate, spending most of their time staring at the ceiling. When they were discharged and it was time to return to Sobhanu's house at Harding Cottage, Narri protested, 'I will not go to that house. I want to go back to the village.'

Sanju nodded in agreement. 'Chacha, please send a message to my parents, they will take us to our village,' he pleaded.

Sobhanu and his friends spent a long time explaining to the young men that the ghost would never enter the house.

'I told you he is a kind soul. He only reacted because you disturbed him, but he still spared your lives. He will not trouble you if you promise to stay away from him,' Bhola explained.

Hurt and frightened, with plaster casts on their limbs, Sanju and Narri reached Harding Cottage. The once adventurous friends were now haunted by their encounter, their bravado replaced by a deep-seated apprehension. The shadows seemed longer and darker, the nights colder, and the memory of the ghost's crimson eyes lingered in their minds. Their fear intensified as night fell and peaked around midnight. They chanted Hanuman Chalisa several times each day in a bid to ward off the spirit of the tall man.

Apart from grappling with their fear, they also had to endure Sobhanu's anger, who cursed them daily for their foolhardy actions.

'I told you to stay indoors and not torment the spirit. But you didn't care to listen. Are you happy now?' He would grumble.

Sanju and Narri could only lower their eyes apologetically, their bravado replaced by a deep regret.

It took the two men a few months to heal completely. Their plasters were removed and they were finally able to move normally again. They felt much better mentally as well. The terror of that night had begun to fade, replaced by a cautious optimism. They started moving out of the house in search of a job but were careful to return to its sanctuary by evening.

One evening, several friends of Sobhanu had come to his house for drinks. Sanju and Narri sat in one corner, listening to their boisterous chatter. Over a few drinks, the conversation inevitably veered towards the ghost of the tall man. With a mischievous grin, one of the men turned to Sanju. 'So,' he asked with mock concern, 'I hope you haven't had any more encounters with your ghostly friend?'

Sanju, his face flushed with anger, was about to retort

when Bhola stepped in. 'Don't listen to him. I am sure you will not have any more encounters with the ghost.' He turned to the two young men and added, 'Now that you're feeling better, we'll go and meet Miss Emily. She knows a lot about the tall man's ghost, and meeting her will dispel all your apprehensions.'

Bhola told Sanju and Narri that Miss Emily had her roots in the United Kingdom. A teacher by profession, she had remained in India even after Independence due to her love for the country. True to his word, he led the two young men to Miss Emily's house a few days later.

'How do you know Miss Emily, Bhola uncle?' Sanju asked, enroute to her house.

'I used to be the caretaker of her house,' Bhola replied with a smile.

Miss Emily was the picture of tranquillity as she sat ensconced in a plush armchair, her aged hands deftly manoeuvring knitting needles. Her silver hair was neatly tied into a bun and a pair of round spectacles perched on her nose. Her fair face bore deep wrinkles, each line a testament to the long and rich life she had lived. Her eyes, though aged, still sparkled with wisdom.

'Welcome, boys. Bhola told me all about you.' Her voice was soft and melodious.

Sanju and Narri immediately felt at ease.

'Thank you for agreeing to meet us, ma'am,' Sanju replied.

After the elementary introductions, Miss Emily informed that she used to teach at Elmwood School and had retired a few years ago. 'The very same school, boys, where the tall spirit you were following disappeared at the gate,' she added with a touch of humour.

Sanju and Narri were stunned.

'Ma'am, who is the tall man? Why is his soul not at peace? Why does he keep going to the school?' Narri asked in one breath.

'Calm down, boys,' she said. 'I will tell you all about Mr Benedict.'

Sanju's eyes widened in surprise. 'Mr Benedict?' He echoed, his voice filled with curiosity.

'Yes, it's the spirit of Mr Benedict you've been seeing,' Miss Emily confirmed in a sombre tone.

With a deep sigh, she added, 'It is a tragic tale of a noble soul...'

'Mr Benedict had been teaching at the Elmwood School since 1910. He was much loved by his pupils and was a respected figure in Mussoorie. He was a quiet man with a gentle demeanour and his dedication to the children was unparalleled. He was more than just a teacher; he was a mentor, a friend to the students,' she said. 'He also had good knowledge of medicine and took care of sick students. There are countless stories about him staying up late to tend to sick kids.'

Miss Emily paused for a moment—lost in thought—before continuing.

Mr Benedict lived a solitary life in a small cottage down the spur. His life was a testament to selfless service, but his death was shrouded in mystery and sorrow.

One stormy night, past midnight—after Mr Benedict had retired to his cottage—a peon from the school reached his house and asked him to come to the school immediately as a little girl had fallen down the stairs and was bleeding profusely. The peon told him that the doctor was not in town and therefore Mr Benedict was required to tend to the girl.

Mr Benedict asked the peon to return to the school, warm some water and boil the syringes, while he got dressed and followed suit. As Mr Benedict hurried to the school, tragedy struck.

'Although nobody knows the details for sure, it is believed that he slipped on the narrow, rain-drenched road and fell into the gorge below...' Miss Emily's voice trailed off.

Meanwhile, back at the school, the matrons at the hostel anxiously awaited Mr Benedict's arrival. Their efforts to stop the little girl's bleeding proved futile and without timely medical intervention, she tragically succumbed to her wounds.

'His body was found the next morning, lifeless and cold. The students, teachers and the entire community mourned his death deeply, and his funeral was attended by hundreds,' Miss Emily's eyes were moist as she narrated the event.

A few years later, as Mr Benedict's memory had just begun to fade, strange occurrences rekindled them.

Many residents reported seeing a spectral figure after midnight, dressed in a dark robe, walking from

Mr Benedict's residence to Elmwood School. The sightings were always the same—a tall, bearded figure, moving urgently with his head bowed.

Miss Emily paused, her eyes distant.

'The description mirrored Mr Benedict rushing towards the school; just as he must have on that fateful night.'

'Is that why we saw him entering the school gate?' Sanju enquired.

'Yes, my boy. That is his nocturnal routine. I guess he feels responsible for the death of the girl and remains around to keep a watch on the campus. Over the years, numerous incidents have occurred that seem to indicate that Mr Benedict is protecting the children like a guardian angel.'

Miss Emily spoke of a fateful evening when a young girl, walking around the campus with her friends, accidentally lost her footing and slipped off the edge of a cliff.

Sanju interrupted, 'And she also lost her life like Mr Benedict!'

Miss Emily shook her head, 'No Sanju, she survived with minor injuries. It was a miracle!'

'How is that possible?' Narri was incredulous.

'Apparently, her clothes caught on a tree branch and prevented a fatal fall,' Miss Emily explained. 'But the child's own account was the most astonishing part.'

She leaned forward, her voice filled with wonder. 'She claimed that a bearded man caught her hand and reassured her by saying that nothing would happen. She

described him as a comforting presence, holding her until help arrived.'

Sanju scoffed, 'Could be the child's imagination.'

Miss Emily smiled.

'Only if it was a one-off incident.'

She recounted another incident when a school group went on a picnic to Hathipaon. There, one boy got separated from the group and his absence was only discovered upon returning to the school. Panic-stricken, the teachers decided to rush back to Hathipaon to search for the child. However, they had barely reached the school gate when they saw the boy entering the premises. 'He claimed that a bearded man found him in the forest, calmed him down, and brought him back,' she said.

She shared yet another incident when, one night, a student developed a very high fever. The matron had barely asked the peon to summon the doctor from his house when the doctor arrived unexpectedly. Both the matron and the peon were astonished.

A smile crept across Miss Emily's face as she continued.

'The doctor said that a bearded man arrived at his house and asked him to come to the school to treat a very sick child.'

'But ma'am, how do you know all this?' Narri asked.

This time, Miss Emily's smile was sad.

'When I joined Elmwood School in the early 1940s, years after Mr Benedict's passing, I heard these stories first-hand. I even witnessed miraculous events that hinted at his continued presence.'

Her voice trembled as she continued, 'I've seen his spirit roaming the school grounds at night, protecting the children he loved.'

Tears welled up in her eyes as she addressed the two men, 'You committed a grave sin by tormenting such a noble soul.'

Sanju and Narri were filled with remorse. Dropping to their knees, they begged Miss Emily for forgiveness.

'Not me,' she advised gently, 'you must seek the forgiveness of Mr Benedict.'

Several decades have passed since this incident occurred. Sanju has long since gone to meet his maker—perhaps he has also met Mr Benedict in person! Narri, on the other hand, is still around. Now an old man, he remains quite lively for his age. Whenever he finds a good audience, he still loves to narrate the tale of Mr Benedict. He is easy to recognize—his missing front teeth give him away whenever he smiles.

As for the spirit of Mr Benedict, maybe he still follows his nocturnal routine. Maybe the new chowkidar of Harding Cottage has seen his spirit!

But of late I have not heard anything about Mr Benedict.

If you happen to encounter him on his nightly vigils, do let me know!

# The Human Oil Extractors

The year was 1944.

It was a splendid autumn morning, the bright sunshine offering a welcome respite from the chill that heralded the approach of winter. The crisp air carried the invigorating scent of fallen leaves and damp earth. A gentle breeze rustled through the leaves of the oak and wild chestnut trees that surrounded the tiny cottage located above the Christ Church.

Dr G sat in the veranda of the cottage, leisurely sipping tea and enjoying the breath-taking panorama of the Doon valley stretched out below.

The physician, in his early forties, exuded a striking presence with his lean physique, fair complexion and sharp features. His neatly trimmed moustache and thick black-rimmed spectacles added an air of intellectual intensity. His voice, deep and resonant, commanded attention and respect, while his impeccable attire—a three-piece suit adorned with a red rosebud in the lapel—spoke of his refined tastes.

'Thank God there is no house visit* today,' he thought with a sigh of relief.

---

*In those days doctors often made house visits to respond to medical emergencies.

The town only had a handful of doctors, and Dr G—the most renowned and respected of the lot—was in high demand. Such moments of leisure were rare for him.

A sudden knock at the door broke the morning silence. 'Spoke too soon,' murmured the doctor with a hint of resignation. He called out to his wife to see who was at the door.

'It's Rahim *bhaiya*,' the doctor's wife shouted from the door.

'Send him to the verandah and make his favourite tea with lots of ginger,' Dr G instructed.

Rahim Baksh, his close friend, strode into the verandah and settled comfortably on a garden chair after the usual exchange of pleasantries.

Despite his busy schedule, Dr G enjoyed the occasional interactions with Rahim, who regaled him with all the news and gossip circulating around town.

'Doctor *saheb*,' Rahim began immediately, his voice filled with intrigue, 'there are a lot of strange things happening in our town these days.'

Knowing his penchant for gossip and his tendency to exaggerate, the doctor responded casually, 'Oh? Like what?'

'People are disappearing,' Rahim declared in a hushed tone. 'Anyone who ventures out at night...simply vanishes without a trace.'

'Perhaps they are simply escaping from their wives for some peace,' Dr G quipped, a wry smile playing on his lips.

After finishing his tea, Rahim departed and Dr G made his way to the clinic—nestled within his cozy cottage—to attend to his patients.

Dr G had almost forgotten about this conversation until, about a week later, Captain Gurbaksh Singh, a retired army official, came for consultation.

'Doctor saheb,' Singh declared in alarm, 'strange things are happening in our town. People are disappearing at night!'

The words jolted Dr G's memory, reminding him of what Rahim had told him earlier.

'Captain, someone else had also mentioned the same thing, but I did not take him seriously.'

'No sir,' Singh insisted, 'this is a grave matter. Ram Lal's servant has been missing for two weeks now, and Lala Bishambar Das's servant vanished a week ago. Even a porter who I regularly hired has vanished without a trace.'

'Something is terribly wrong,' he concluded, his voice tinged with unease.

Dr G, a stoic man, would never have readily believed such tales. But he held deep respect for Captain Gurbaksh Singh—a highly decorated soldier and a fearless individual.

'What do you think is happening?'

'Everyone is clueless,' Singh replied with a sigh. 'Some of us even went to the police to file a report, but that fat inspector was too casual about it, brushing it off as nothing.'

'Hmmm...' Dr G muttered, lost deep in thought.

That evening, as soon as his clinic hours concluded, Dr G rushed towards Picture Palace, eager to meet Rahim. He was troubled by the strange disappearances reported in the town.

Rahim had a prominent shop on the bustling Mall Road near Picture Palace. While his staff managed the business, Rahim kept himself busy by gossiping with residents and officials who frequented the Mall, not to mention his long chats with the neighbouring shopkeepers. Thus, he managed to stay remarkably well-informed about all the happenings in town.

'What brings you here, doctor saheb? Are you out visiting a patient?' Rahim greeted in his usual carefree tone.

But the doctor was in no mood for pleasantries. 'Gurbaksh saheb came to my clinic today,' he said. 'He also told me about the disappearing men!'

A triumphant smile spread across Rahim's face.

'Do you believe me now?' He asked with a hint of vindication in his voice. 'Yes, yes,' Dr G admitted impatiently. 'But how are they disappearing? Any idea?'

Rahim took the doctor's arm and led him to the back of his shop where a small desk and chairs were kept. He motioned Dr G to take a seat and settled into his chair behind the desk.

'I have discussed this with many people... The disappearances are the work of ghosts,' Rahim whispered, leaning towards the doctor.

'What? That is preposterous!'

'Doctor saheb, it's *true*,' Rahim pleaded, his voice trembling slightly. 'Looking out of their windows, many residents have seen dark shadows moving around at night.'

Dr G's eyes widened in disbelief. 'Shadows? What may these be?'

'These are the evil spirits that are abducting people. They vanish as quickly as they appear.'

Dr G's scepticism was palpable.

'As a medical practitioner, I find it difficult to believe in ghosts. Could there be another explanation for the disappearances?'

Rahim remained firm in his belief. 'None that I know.'

The two men sat in silence for the rest of the evening, sipping the tea that Rahim had ordered. The quiet was broken only by the clinking of cups and an occasional sigh. As Dr G made his way back home, Rahim's words echoed in his mind, casting a shadow of unease.

'Is our town truly haunted by evil spirits? What are these dark shadows?'

He shivered as the unsettling conversation with Rahim replayed in his mind. Yet, the rational part of his mind rejected the notion of evil spirits. 'This must be the handiwork of some gang of thugs who have arrived from the plains to loot the residents,' he reasoned.

Over the next few weeks, residents from all walks of life came to Dr G for consultation. He also made a number of house calls to respond to medical emergencies. With each patient, he subtly attempted to bring up the topic of the disappearances. He would casually ask, 'So, what is new in our town?' 'How are things going around here?' 'Any interesting news in town lately?'

Several patients brought up the disappearances in town and some even hinted at ghosts or evil spirits being responsible.

'Doctor saheb, our town is tormented by ghosts who haunt the streets after dark and make people disappear,' one patient fearfully confided.

Another patient warned him not to go out at night. 'Black shadows wander the streets and abduct people, who are never found.'

'Maybe they are not evil spirits but a gang of miscreants operating in the town,' Dr G would insinuate. But every patient he posed this alternative to would fervently refuse to believe him.

Despite his scepticism, Dr G couldn't ignore the growing unease gripping the townspeople. The fear was palpable. Residents avoided going out after dark, and the town's workforce dwindled as the workers—who were disappearing on a daily basis—decided to seek employment elsewhere.

Rahim came to meet the doctor several times during this period and each time reinforced his theory of ghosts lurking around the town. Dr G tried to reason with him, but that only led to arguments between them.

Worried by the unsettling events unfolding around him, Dr G also started avoiding house visits after dark.

One evening, while the doctor was taking a

well-deserved break after a particularly demanding day of work, a loud knock startled him from his slumber.

Moments later, the doctor's wife appeared and told him that Mr Walker's servant was at the door, requesting to meet him.

Alan Walker was a retired civil servant and a close friend of Dr G. A widower, he lived alone in a large house on Camel's Back Road and grappled with multiple health problems which Dr G attended to.

Deeply concerned about his friend, Dr G immediately leaped out of his bed and hastily got dressed, instructing his wife to ask the servant to wait outside. He put some essentials in his physician's bag and rushed out of the house, and his bag was promptly picked up by the servant waiting outside. Together, they made their way towards Mr Walker's house.

They reached at dusk and found Mr Walker writhing in agony on the bed, holding his stomach. Dr G dutifully attended to his friend—administering an injection and giving medicines to alleviate his pain—and waited patiently by his side for several hours until Mr Walker showed some signs of relief.

As he was leaving, Mr Walker insisted that his servant escort him home. But Dr G declined, stating that he would prefer the servant remained by his side and attended to his needs.

However, as he walked out to the pitch-black night outside, the doctor was awash with fearful regret. The thought of the recent disappearances and the rumours of evil lurking in the shadows echoed in his mind.

'I should have let the servant escort me home,' he thought.

But, being a proud man, he could not bring himself to go back inside and request the servant's company. In his hurry, Dr G had left his watch at home. But judging by the darkness, he estimated that it was around 9.00 p.m.

'Everyone advised me to avoid going out after dark. I should have left Mr Walker's house earlier.'

The deserted Camel's Back Road stretched before him, shrouded in darkness. Dr G took out his flashlight and its beam cut a swathe through the night, revealing a small circle of ground ahead. He steeled himself with a deep breath and began the long walk home. The silence was punctuated by the crunch of gravel under his feet and the frantic beating of his heart.

Every rustle of leaves or snap of twigs sent a jolt through him, conjuring images of the dark shadows that had been tormenting the town. Occasionally, he would whirl around—piercing the darkness behind him with the beam of his flashlight—to check that he was not being followed.

A brisk ten minutes' walk brought him close to the point where the Camel's Back Road joined the Mall Road. A wave of relief washed over him.

'Thank goodness! The Mall Road is well-lit, and the police guard should be on patrol.'

The thought had barely crossed his mind when two shadows emerged from the bushes by the roadside. They were of small stature, cloaked in what seemed to be black robes with hoods obscuring their faces.

Before a startled Dr G could react or gather enough wits to turn back and run, the duo pounced upon him with surprising agility and pinned him to the ground.

Dr G was paralyzed with fear—his chest tightened and his heart threatened to leap out of his throat. He desperately tried to resist his assailants but found their grip to be hopelessly unyielding.

The assailants were about to cover his mouth with a cloth to prevent him from shouting for help, when Dr G mustered all his strength and managed to shout, 'I'm a doctor! I'm a doctor!'

This proclamation made the duo abruptly halt their assault. They quickly opened his bag and rifled through its contents. When its contents concurred with his claim, the assailants abandoned him and vanished into the darkness.

Relieved beyond measure, Dr G scrambled to his feet. His heart still racing, he looked around to make sure his assailants had indeed left, and seeing no trace of them, bolted towards the Mall Road.

He had never felt such overwhelming gratitude as he did when he finally reached the well-lit Mall Road. Exhausted and trembling, he collapsed under the comforting glow of streetlights.

'Thank God...' He muttered, voice trembling with relief.

The halo of the streetlights enveloped Dr G as he lay on the Mall Road. His legs felt like lead, and the rush of adrenaline that had fuelled his escape now left him utterly drained. As he stared blankly at the ground, a constable on patrol noticed him and approached.

'Are you alright, sir?' He asked in a concerned voice. Dr G, still visibly shaken, recounted his terrifying ordeal to the policeman. However, judging by his reaction, he didn't seem entirely convinced.

'Perhaps the darkness played tricks on you,' the constable suggested in a compassionate yet sceptical tone. Without arguing, Dr G simply requested the constable to accompany him back to the spot where he had left his belongings. Next morning he called for Rahim and narrated the entire incident to him.

'Rahim, one thing I have realized is that these shadows are not ghosts but flesh-and-blood mortals,' he declared firmly.

'Although their faces were concealed, I could discern that they had small, round faces. That and their short stature suggest they are people of South Asian origin,' Dr G added with conviction.

'I don't doubt you, my friend,' Rahim replied, his brow furrowed in thought. 'But if they are men, then *who* are they? And *why* are they abducting people?'

'Let's go to the police inspector and ask him to investigate,' the doctor suggested. Rahim scoffed.

'Futile,' he muttered. 'Inspector Hick won't lift a finger.'

Despite Rahim's reservations, they went to Inspector Hick to register a complaint. A short, portly man with a round face, Hick listened to the doctor's account with a detached air and reluctantly registered a complaint, but expressed hesitation about increasing the night patrols, citing limited manpower.

'I told you! Hick won't do anything,' Rahim grumbled as they descended the stairs of the police station.

'Let him go to hell! We will uncover the truth of this gang on our own,' Dr G's frustration echoed through the dimly lit stairwell.

Thus, they set out to uncover the truth behind the abductions that plagued their town. At the doctor's suggestion, they also took Captain Singh into confidence and sought his help. The three men decided to conduct some research at the Mussoorie Library, hoping to uncover clues about the assailants. Gurbaksh, being retired, readily agreed to spend his time poring over old manuscripts, books and journals. Meanwhile, Rahim and Dr G leveraged their connections with the townsfolk to gather information from the residents—especially the elderly. They hoped to find someone who might hold a clue about the mysterious figures and their motives.

Months passed without any clue. One evening, when Dr G was about to close his clinic for the day, a diminutive, dark-skinned old man, clad in tattered garments, arrived, seeking medical attention.

Observing the man's condition, the doctor quickly deduced his dire financial situation. But he examined the man without remark and provided him with the necessary medication. The man's voice trembled in hesitation as he asked, 'What is your fee, doctor saheb?'

Dr G, feeling a wave of pity for him, knew that the man couldn't afford to pay for the consultation or the medication. He leaned back in his creaking chair, clasped his hands behind his head and offered a warm smile. 'There is no fee,' he said kindly.

The man's face lit up with relief and gratitude, his eyes welling up with tears at the doctor's kindness.

'What is your name? What do you do?' The doctor asked, trying to lighten the mood.

The man replied that his name was Naktu Ram. He used to work as a chowkidar but lost his job years ago. Now he survived by doing daily labour and odd jobs for shopkeepers.

'How did you lose your job?'

'I worked at a brewery for many years. Due to losses, the brewery was closed down and I lost my job,' Naktu explained sadly. Then his tone shifted slightly. 'But in a way it was good that the brewery closed, sir. A lot of bad things happened there.' His eyes briefly darted away, as if recalling unpleasant memories.

Dr G was filled with curiosity.

'What things happened there?'

Naktu Ram fell silent, his gaze fixed on the ground as if regretting his words.

'Don't worry, my friend,' Dr G reassured him gently. 'I'm not one to spread gossip. I'm asking because I'm curious about interesting stories. Consider it a payment for your treatment.'

'Sir, I am afraid of the *Telis*,' Naktu Ram stammered, his voice barely a whisper. 'If word gets out that I spoke about the horrors at the brewery, I fear they might come after me.'

'Telis! Who are they? Tell me more, my friend, don't be afraid,' Dr G implored, his curiosity piqued.

Naktu Ram hesitated, then said in a hushed tone, 'The Telis are the ones who are abducting people from the streets.'

He said that the Telis abducted their victims at night and made them unconscious. Bound in large sacks, the victims were carried to their hideout in the forests near the brewery.

'Sir, I have seen them carrying the sacks to an old dilapidated building in the forests near the brewery,' Naktu confessed, his voice trembling.

When he first noticed these black-robed people carrying a sack towards the forest, he had become curious and discreetly followed them to their hideout.

'At their hideout, I peeped through a large window in the stone wall. What I saw shook me to the core,' Naktu revealed, his voice thick with emotion.

'A large fire burnt on the floor and a man was hung upside down over it, while several black-robed shapes stood surrounding him,' Naktu recounted. 'The poor man screamed in agony, begging for mercy. But these fiends showed no compassion.'

'But why would they do that?' Dr G's face was a mask of horror and bewilderment.

'It is said that through this process, the victim's body fat would drip down from his head into a vessel placed beside the fire. This fat is highly valuable for its use in treating war wounds,' Naktu explained.

'Naktu, I hope you are telling the truth,' the doctor's voice was stern.

'Sir, why would I lie to you?' Naktu replied earnestly, his voice tinged with hurt. 'You have been so kind to me.'

The doctor nodded and motioned Naktu to continue.

He explained that after the fat was extracted, the Telis burnt the bodies at their hideout or disposed of them in the furnaces at the brewery.

'The brewery became a forsaken place because of the number of dead bodies disposed there. Cursed by the dead, it ultimately closed down.'

He explained that during his nocturnal vigils, he frequently witnessed the Telis transporting people to their hideout, but never dared to venture near their lair again.

'I was terrified that I would also meet the same fate as the other victims if the Telis discovered my intrusion,' Naktu's voice trembled with lingering fear.

It was already dark outside when Naktu left the clinic. But long after he was gone, Dr G remained seated inside—lost in thought—grappling with the horrifying reality that Naktu had revealed. His reverie was only broken when his wife entered the clinic, reminding him that dinner was ready.

That whole night, Dr G could not sleep a wink, unsettled by the ghastly events that had been plaguing the quiet town. The image of innocent victims suffering ghastly fates at the hands of the Telis haunted him. The following morning, Dr G met with Rahim and Gurbaksh. He shared the horrifying details he had learned—the existence of the Telis, their gruesome practices and their hidden lair near the abandoned brewery. He carefully omitted Naktu Ram's name for the fear of the man's safety.

His friends were aghast to learn about these gory details.

'They're kidnapping people to extract oil from their bodies!' Rahim exclaimed, his voice filled with a mix of horror and disbelief. 'Have you heard anything about "human oil", doctor?'

'Sounds far-fetched,' Dr G replied, his scepticism evident. Being a man of science, he was hesitant to accept the existence of something as fantastical as human oil, let alone the possibility of extracting it.

'It seems the Telis have the tacit support of the government; otherwise, how could this sinister operation continue for so long?' Gurbaksh said, his voice filled with righteous anger.

'Calm down, Captain. We have no proof to accuse the government,' Dr G said.

'We must put an end to this, doctor saheb,' Gurbaksh declared.

Enraged and appalled, the three friends immediately marched to the police station to confront Inspector Hick. They informed him about the Telis, their gruesome activities and the location of their hideout near the abandoned brewery.

'Do you have any eyewitnesses?' The inspector asked, raising his brows in scepticism.

Fearing for Naktu Ram's safety, Dr G decided to keep his identity a secret. 'No, inspector,' he replied sheepishly.

'Sounds damn far-fetched,' Hick dismissively declared. 'However, I'll instruct my officers to look into it.'

Dr G and his friends followed up with the inspector several times, but each time they were met with the same frustrating response:

'We are investigating.'

'I think he's in cahoots with the Telis,' Rahim muttered angrily one day. 'Or maybe his entire government is sponsoring these monsters?'

Frustrated, the friends thought of approaching the higher police officials and even going to the press to expose the sinister deeds of the Telis. But before they could act, India's Independence was declared and along with the British, the Telis also disappeared, never to be heard from again.

During the 1990s, Dr G, a nonagenarian by then, told me of his experiences with the Telis. Baffled and intrigued by his narrative, I immediately set off to do some research on them. I stumbled upon some old books that mentioned cases of missing porters and coolies in the 1850s and 1860s. The books mentioned that townsfolk were being abducted by 'Telis', aka 'human oil extractors', who extracted 'oil' from humans. The fear of Telis led to a large-scale exodus of porters from the town. The British tried to deny the occurrences in a bid to woo the porters to stay in the town.

I also came across a travelogue[*] by Lady Constance Frederica Gordon Cumming, who visited Mussoorie in the 1870s. She observed:

> To a population thus dependent upon the multitude of human workers, any cause that diminishes the supply is a serious matter. Imagine, then, the effect of a story having, some years ago, been circulated among the hill tribes that the Europeans required a vast supply of "Pahari oil," and intended to take every hill man, woman, or child, whom they could catch, and hang them up by the heels before a big fire in order to extract their oil! This story was universally believed that all the coolies ran away from Massourie (read Mussoorie), and were only persuaded by slow degrees of return; and for months they continued to work tremblingly, still believing in danger.

While Lady Constance believed that the word going around town about the Telis was just a 'story', she was perhaps just being a mouthpiece for the British.

Did the Telis actually exist? Were they humans or supernatural beings? Did they actually abduct people and extract human oil? Why was human oil extracted?

---

*Cumming, C.F.G., *From the Hebrides to the Himalayas: Volume II*, Sampson Low, Marston, Searle and Rivington, London, 1876, p. 280.

Questions such as these, though unanswered, are still pondered over at leisure, albeit amongst a small section of citizenry today—the elderly who have heard fables from their fathers and grandfathers about the Telis.

# The Old Mines

Sameer, a native of Bihar, had spent nearly two decades trapped in the monotonous grind of a Delhi office. The stress at the lowly paid job and Delhi's relentless pollution and traffic had worn him down. An orphan since youth, with no family ties to anchor him, his life had become a solitary existence.

One day, he decided that he had had enough of this miserable life. Leaving everything behind, he decided to venture into the hills!

The crisp mountain air filled Sameer's lungs as he stepped out of the bus at Gandhi Chowk. Sameer had imagined a world untouched by Delhi's cacophony. He booked a modest lodge and set out to explore the town, only to find that even here the hustle and bustle of tourists threatened to shatter the peace he sought.

'This place is as crowded and noisy as Delhi,' Sameer muttered, sipping his tea at a small shop nestled behind the library building at Gandhi Chowk. Over the past two weeks, he had become a regular at the shop, forging friendships with the owner and other patrons.

A man sitting in one corner and slurping tea loudly suggested, 'If you're looking for peace and quiet, you should get away from the main town.'

Sameer thought the man's advice was useful. Without delay, he checked out of the guesthouse, slung his rucksack over his shoulders, and set off on foot towards the outskirts of Mussoorie.

For days, he wandered around, seeking a peaceful place to settle down. He stayed at various homestays on the periphery of the town and even spent a night under the open sky. Then, one morning, he stumbled upon a cluster of dilapidated buildings a short distance from the main road. Surrounded by a dense patch of forest and overlooking a stark, barren mountain, the place exuded an aura of solitude.

'This place looks amazing,' Sameer thought as he explored the buildings. 'These buildings seem to have been abandoned, and no one would mind if I settled in one small room.'

He contracted a carpenter to fix the doors and windows in one of the rooms to create a makeshift abode. He also found a spring nearby that could serve as a source of fresh water.

He soon realized that the area attracted tourists, especially young people from Dehradun who used the nearby road to reach popular tourist spots. A few even ventured into the buildings. Recognizing an opportunity, Sameer immediately opened a small eatery serving tea and snacks. A few weeks passed peacefully.

'This is the life I always wanted,' he thought contentedly.

Then one day, an elderly person from a nearby village happened to stop by his eatery. The curious villager made enquiries about his origins and also asked where he was living in Mussoorie.

'I live in the deserted buildings down below,' Sameer replied casually.

This information changed the old man's demeanour dramatically. His face distorted in surprise and fear, and he shouted, 'Leave the building, find some other place to stay!'

Sameer was taken aback by the intensity of the man's reaction. 'Why do you say that, chacha?' He asked, trying to understand the source of his fear.

The villager's expression turned grave. 'Many have seen and heard things here that cannot be explained. These buildings were the offices of the Old Mines where many workers died. Their spirits still linger here. It's not safe for anyone to stay.'

With that he turned and hurried away.

This sinister warning made Sameer a bit apprehensive. However, a part of him suspected an ulterior motive. Maybe the villager was trying to scare him away for personal reasons. So, the next day he went to the nearby village to investigate and spoke to several people. Everyone advised against staying in those buildings.

He learnt that the Old Mines were regarded as one of the most haunted sites in Mussoorie. Its sinister reputation was linked to the tragic demise of 38 miners who were entombed alive in a landslide caused by an

accidental explosion in 1968. Though the mine ceased
operations in 1988, its macabre history continues to
unfold. A chilling array of subsequent fatalities, including
a wife's murderous act, a young man's despairing suicide,
a string of fatal car accidents and even a chopper crash
fuelled the belief in malevolent forces haunting the site.
People speculated that the mine's concentrated negative
energy was a catalyst for these untimely deaths.

Sameer learned that the abandoned buildings once
housed the offices, residences and hospital of the
mine, while the actual mining area was located about a
kilometre beyond them.

'As darkness descends, this place transforms into a
realm of terror—no one dares go there—especially to
the mining site which is rumoured to be more evil,'
Ram Lal warned.

After hearing these accounts, Sameer returned to his
room, dejected and fearful. 'I should leave this place,'
he thought. But another, more defiant voice countered,
'Where will you go, Sameer? You have no home and
little savings!'

The night was a restless one for Sameer, his mind
racing with the conflicting thoughts. Should he heed
the villagers' warnings and flee, or should he stay and
confront his fears? As dawn broke, he made a decision—a
decision born of both courage and desperation.

He would stay.

A few days passed uneventfully and Sameer's anxieties
gradually subsided.

'The villagers were unnecessarily making up stories,' he thought, shaking his head at their superstitious fears.

One bright and sunny morning, Sameer sat in the courtyard outside his room, savouring his breakfast. The golden sunlight danced across his face, filling him with a sense of peace and contentment.

Suddenly, a murder of crows descended from the sky, their black wings casting ominous shadows as they landed on the old building's roof—their raucous cawing shattered the tranquillity of the courtyard. Moments later, they descended further to the ground, their beady eyes fixed on the plate in Sameer's hand.

'Shooo!' Sameer yelled. But they were undeterred, their audacity growing with each passing moment. In a desperate attempt to scare them off, Sameer waved his arm which accidentally brushed against a crow, triggering a chorus of angry caws. Several crows flew menacingly close to Sameer as if threatening to strike him—their sharp beaks and talons glinting in the sunlight.

Dropping his plate in terror, Sameer bolted for the safety of his room, slamming the door shut behind him. His heart pounded in his chest as he caught his breath. 'I've never seen crows behave like that,' he thought, feeling slightly unnerved.

And from that day onwards, strange events began to unfold.

One night, he was startled by a knock on his door, but upon opening it he found no one. 'The wind must be playing tricks,' Sameer mused as he stood at the threshold with the door ajar.

The following night, after midnight, he heard the knock again. But just like before he found no one at the door. Sameer started to grow increasingly baffled. 'Is someone playing a prank?' He wondered.

Then Sameer started hearing footsteps late into the night, as if several people were pacing restlessly outside his door. This became a nightly ritual and Sameer was now sure that something was amiss and began to suspect that these were paranormal occurrences.

Along with the regular knocks on his door and footsteps outside his room, he also heard loud sounds of shovels scraping against the earth, as if the miners were still at work in the abandoned mine. One night, as Sameer stood outside his room, he noticed a bright light in the forest. Since there was no human habitation in that dense forest, Sameer was baffled by its presence.

Then, over the course of the next month, a couple of tragic road accidents occurred near the mines. A vehicle veered off the road, claiming two lives, and a biker was found dead at the bottom of a deep gorge near the mine entrance. Sameer realized that the villagers were right— the place was indeed haunted. Fear gripped him, but his unwavering faith in God provided solace. 'God had a reason for sending me here,' he reassured himself. 'He prompted me to stay here and now he will protect me.'

At that moment, a memory surfaced in Sameer's mind—a cherished talisman bequeathed to him by his late father. He recalled his father's words: 'This talisman belonged to your forefathers. Hanging it behind the front door will protect your home from thieves and evil spirits.'

Driven by a newfound sense of hope, Sameer rummaged through his belongings and retrieved a small, oval-shaped piece of bone, bleached white by time and handling. It was etched with intricate symbols and patterns, their meanings lost to the ages. A small hole had been drilled through the top, allowing it to be threaded onto a piece of twine for hanging.

He quickly located a nail and, with a sense of reverence, affixed the talisman behind the door. The act of hanging it brought about a wave of relief and reassurance.

'Thank God, I remembered this at the right time,' Sameer whispered to himself, a flicker of hope warming his troubled spirit. 'I am sure this will protect me.'

With the talisman in place, Sameer felt a measure of safety within the confines of his room. He consciously avoided venturing out after sunset, dedicating more of his time to prayers. But outside his room, a series of strange and frightening incidents continued to unfold. The first incident involved a doctor from Delhi who had come to Mussoorie and had stopped by Sameer's shack with his family. The doctor's towering height and broad, muscular build gave him a commanding presence, more reminiscent of an athlete than a medical practitioner. His deliberate stride and impeccable posture exuded a self-assuredness that seemed to teeter on the edge of arrogance.

The doctor casually asked about the deserted building. 'Is that building up for sale?' He asked in a condescending tone.

'Sir, that building is haunted,' Sameer replied, his voice steady despite the doctor's dismissive attitude.

'What rubbish! I am a doctor; I do not believe in the supernatural,' the doctor declared. 'Show me around, I'm not afraid. Ghosts are nonsense.'

Agitated and angered by the doctor's response, Sameer challenged him. 'If you're so confident, come to the building at night and see for yourself.'

Hearing the sound of a car at midnight, Sameer, who did not want to venture outside, reluctantly came out of his room.

The doctor had arrived in a swanky car and brought his two sons and wife along. As the doctor emerged out of his car, Sameer saw that his family refused to come out. He beckoned to Sameer and asked him to accompany him inside the buildings. When Sameer refused, the doctor laughed mockingly and marched inside one of them.

But he burst out moments later—terror etched on his face—and rushed to his car. He frantically fumbled with the door handle but it wouldn't budge. With shaking hands, he tried to use his keys, but the door remained stubbornly locked. His family, trapped inside, pounded on the windows and shouted in panic.

The car's electronics had inexplicably malfunctioned.

The doctor turned to Sameer with a desperate look on his face and handed him the car keys. Recognizing the supernatural elements at work, Sameer briefly knelt in prayer, then pressed the unlock button. The car responded with a click. The doctor stared at Sameer in confusion and awe.

'Sir,' Sameer said solemnly, 'your disregard for the supernatural has provoked the spirits.' He urged the doctor to depart without delay.

That day, Sameer realized that the spirits could be subdued through prayer. This realization instilled in him a newfound confidence, reducing his fear of the place and its spectral inhabitants. He began to disregard the nocturnal disturbances and no longer hesitated to venture out at night if it was required.

Then, one day, a few students from Haryana came on a camping trip and met Sameer at his shack. One of them introduced himself as Roshan and spoke to Sameer.

'We are looking for a place to camp and this ground in front of the buildings looks scenic and quiet,' he said. 'Do you know if we can camp here?'

Sameer flatly refused. 'You know there is evil in this place and unusual things happen after midnight. You must look for another place to camp.'

'How do you know there is evil here?' Roshan asked.

'Because I live here, and I have witnessed...abnormal activities,' Sameer replied, his voice grave.

Roshan let out a raucous laugh, waving his hand dismissively, and shouted to his friends. 'Guys, the old man is just spinning ghost stories because he does not want us to camp here. There's nothing to be afraid of.'

The students shouted in unison, 'We will camp here, uncle. We are not afraid of ghosts. You just provide us with dinner and breakfast.'

Sameer, recognizing that further warnings would be futile, simply shrugged and resumed his daily tasks.

That night, the students pitched their tents near Sameer's room and started a campfire with wood collected from nearby. Then, fuelled by a mix of bravado and youthful recklessness, they opened a bottle of liquor. As he prepared their dinner in his room, Sameer overheard whispers and muffled laughter drifting in from the campsite.

Once the food was ready, Sameer stepped outside to call the students, who—flushed with alcohol and excitement—greeted him with boisterous cheers. Their laughter echoed through the night.

'Dinner is ready, come inside,' Sameer invited, his voice carrying a hint of concern. But the inebriated students were in no mood to listen.

'We haven't finished our drinks yet, old man,' one of them slurred, raising his glass in a mock toast. 'Come, you also join us. Let's celebrate!'

Looking at the mood of the students, Sameer knew it was pointless to argue and quietly retreated to his room. But he couldn't shake the feeling that this revelry was a prelude to something malevolent. An uneasy shiver ran down his spine.

As he sat down to a solitary meal, he couldn't help but berate himself. 'What a mistake I have made,' he muttered under his breath, pushing the food around his plate. 'Why did I ever allow these foolish students to camp here?'

Meanwhile, out in the courtyard, two students—Roshan and Abhay—decided to explore the crumbling buildings. With arms draped over each other's shoulders, they tipsily ventured into the complex. Laughing loudly and taking selfies in the dark, they passed through the large halls of the first building which was once the office complex of the mine. The beams of the flashlights from their mobile phones illuminated the damp and decaying walls of the empty hall and the accumulated debris of dust and leaves that carpeted the floor.

'Ugh… Nothing interesting here except grime and dust. Let's check the next building,' Roshan suggested with a hint of disappointment in his voice.

The next building was smaller—the two youngsters were unaware that it had once served as a makeshift hospital for the miners. They passed through a small room and entered a small hall. It used to be the general ward where beds were laid out for the injured and sick workers. A sudden unsettling feeling crept over the two friends. The air grew heavy and a chill seemed to seep from the walls.

'It's pretty suffocating in here,' Abhay murmured.

'Oh, don't worry, it's just the smell of damp and decay,' Roshan reassured him, though his own heart pounded faster.

Suddenly, the silence was shattered by the sounds of

men shouting in pain and distress. Eerie wails and cries of 'Help...! Help...!' reverberated through the hall; the voices of the distressed and injured miners were echoing through time.

'G-g-ghos...' Abhay's scream died in his throat, replaced by a strangled gasp. He grabbed Roshan's sleeve in a vice-grip and yanked him towards the door, his eyes wide with terror. Roshan, equally unnerved, allowed himself to be dragged out of the building. The duo burst into the courtyard—their faces pale and breaths coming in ragged gasps—and frantically ran towards their friends, whose voices were raised in drunken song around the bonfire, oblivious of their terror.

'*Ghosts...! GHOSTS!*' Abhay was finally able to cry out in alarm.

The other students paused mid-song and turned to the two figures stumbling towards them. But in their drunken merriment, they mistook Abhay and Roshan's terror for an elaborate prank.

'Nice try, guys!' Someone shouted, raising his glass. 'But you'll have to do better than that to scare us!' His words met with a wave of laughter from the others.

'It's not a joke!' Roshan gasped, clutching his friend's arm. 'We saw...we *heard...*'

Hearing Roshan, who was considered their leader and who never minced words, the group was alarmed. By then, Sameer had also come out of his room. 'What happened, boys?' He enquired, sensing that something was amiss.

'They saw ghosts,' Vimal stammered, in a trembling voice.

Sameer's heart sank as he realized that his worst fears had come true. The dark forces that plagued the Old Mines had manifested again, and this time their malicious intent was strong and palpable. His thoughts were interrupted by a piercing scream ripping through the night. The sound curdled Sameer's blood.

The students had frozen, their eyes widened in horror.

This scream was followed by another loud cry of 'HELP...!'

'Someone is in trouble,' Sameer exclaimed. Instinctively, he grabbed a flashlight and sprinted in the direction of the sound. The students, their fear momentarily forgotten, hesitated for a split second before following Sameer into the darkness.

The scream erupted again—closer this time—followed by a crashing sound. Sameer and the students quickened their pace and soon emerged into a small clearing.

Their flashlights illuminated a horrifying scene.

Many men lay sprawled on the ground, half-buried under a cascade of rocks that appeared to have fallen from the adjacent mountain. Sameer could make out the blood-covered face of some men, while most others seemed to be completely concealed beneath the rubble, only their feet or hands protruding outside.

The men screamed in agony, their pleas for help echoing through the debris.

'Come on, boys, let's get them out of here,' Sameer urged.

As they approached the injured men, a chilling transformation occurred. All of them abruptly emerged from the rocks, their faces and clothes drenched in blood, each gripping a shovel with deadly intent.

'The miners who were buried in the landslides,' Sameer managed to whisper as a cold dread gripped his heart.

Menacingly, the miners, or perhaps their vengeful spirits, advanced towards Sameer and the students. Their eyes gleamed with ominous light, and cruel smiles twisted their grotesque, blood-smeared faces.

Their demonic laughter played a chilling symphony in the darkness.

Sameer and the others stood paralyzed with fear, unable to move as the macabre figures closed in.

Some of them slowly lifted their shovels above their heads, as if to strike.

Sameer, realizing that end was near, started reciting the Hanuman Chalisa loudly and a sudden surge of courage replaced his fear. '*Run...* Come *on!*' He shouted to the students, pivoting and sprinting away as fast as his legs could carry him. Jolted from their stupor, the students followed suit, racing back towards the safety of the buildings.

Through all this, Sameer kept reciting the Hanuman Chalisa.

After running for a while, Sameer risked a glance

over his shoulder, and was astonished to find that the spectral figures had vanished into the thin mountain air. Heaving a sigh of relief, he paused to catch his breath. The students, equally exhausted, stopped beside him, panting and wide-eyed with terror.

'They are gone... We are saved...' Roshan said, his voice regaining its usual confidence.

'Let's go. We won't be out of danger until we reach my room,' Sameer urged.

As the group started moving forward, a massive boulder thundered down the hillside, landing precisely where they had been standing moments before.

'Run!' Everyone shouted, panic-stricken once again. As they sprinted along the narrow path, large and small rocks tumbled down from the ridge above. Miraculously, none of them struck anyone.

As they reached Sameer's room, everyone rushed inside, pushing and shoving in their desperation. Sameer swiftly bolted the door, his hands shaking slightly.

'W-what if th-they come inside?' Abhay struggled to form words.

'No, we are safe here,' Sameer reassured, though his voice betrayed a hint of nervousness. He placed his faith in the talisman, believing it would shield them from harm.

For over an hour, Sameer sat on his bed with his eyes closed and prayed loudly. The students huddled together in the small room—pale-faced and trembling— too terrified to utter a word.

Finally, after finishing the prayers, Sameer broke the silence.

'Boys, we had a lucky escape today! You had angered the spirits by drinking here and making loud noises,' he admonished.

The students hung their faces in shame, the bravado of before completely dissipated. Outside the bolted door, the rhythmic thud of heavy footsteps echoed through the night, punctuated by occasional, bone-chilling wails. After a while, all of them fell into a fitful slumber, their dreams haunted by the night's events.

As dawn broke, Sameer stirred awake. The morning sunlight gently filtered through the gap beneath the door. He looked around the room. Roshan and his companions lay fast asleep on the floor.

Sameer stood up on trembling legs—perhaps the fear and physical exertion of the previous night taking its toll. He carefully navigated his way to the door— through the sprawled mass of sleeping students—opened it a crack and peeped outside. The courtyard, bathed in the soothing warmth of the morning sunlight, offered a sense of calm reassurance.

With renewed courage, he stepped outside but was stopped in his steps.

'Oh my God!'

His voice betrayed a mix of alarm and disbelief.

The two tents pitched by Roshan and his companions had been uprooted and savagely torn—their pieces scattered all across the courtyard. The liquor bottle seemed to have been brutally crushed as if something heavy was thrown upon it; the plastic glasses had met with a similar fate. The rucksacks had been ripped apart and their contents—clothing, toiletries and other personal belongings—strewn, torn and crushed.

'Brutal and vengeful spirits at work... What would they have done to us?'

Sameer shivered with dread.

In that moment he made a firm decision. He would never return to this place. The fear that gripped him was too profound and the events of the night had been too harrowing. 'I will find a room on rent,' he vowed to himself, 'even if it's close to human habitation, even if the surroundings are not as quiet and picturesque as this!'

'At least I will live a life free from fear,' he murmured, 'a life without the constant threat of evil.'

Once the young men woke up and emerged from the room, they were distraught at the ruthlessness with which their belongings had been destroyed.

'Don't worry, boys, at least we are alive!' Sameer declared as he gathered his meagre belongings from the room, making sure not to forget the talisman.

They left the Old Mines together. But the scars of that night would remain etched in their minds forever.

For years following the incident, Sameer would occasionally awaken in cold sweat; he would relive the terror of being pursued by the angry miners in his nightmares, his heart pounding as he desperately ran for his life.

Several years later, I—alongside a group of friends from Delhi—ventured to the Old Mines. Unaware of the site's dark history, we were simply enjoying a leisurely drive when the peaceful and serene surroundings captivated our attention.

'Isn't this a lovely place?'

Ashish's off-hand observation was echoed by the rest of us as we took in the tranquil beauty.

We settled in the courtyard adjacent to the buildings and basked in the warm winter sun, marvelling at the panoramic view of the Doon Valley. The serenity of the place was almost hypnotic, and for a moment, we were lost in the calm atmosphere.

Breaking the silence, I pondered aloud, 'What is this place? Why are these buildings abandoned?'

While my friends engaged in casual banter, curiosity propelled me into the dilapidated buildings. Vast, cavernous halls, devoid of doors or windows, stretched before me, their emptiness accentuated by the absence of any furniture—likely removed when the buildings were abandoned or scavenged by *kabadiwallah*s in the intervening years.

The damp floor was carpeted by oak leaves blown in by relentless winds. Peeling plaster and verdant patches of fungus marred the walls, amplifying the sense of decay and abandonment. Amidst this desolation were 'I love you' messages or creative proclamations with an arrow piercing the heart followed by names of the lovebirds who might have frequented the place to steal some moments of privacy.

As I moved to the next building—a smaller one—a wave of unease washed over me. The air felt heavy and I began to feel claustrophobic. 'Just the smell of decay,' I reasoned, trying to dismiss the growing unease. A sudden, distinct sound of footsteps and crunch of leaves sent a shiver down my spine. Panicked, I rushed out into the sunlight to join my friends who were enjoying their outing.

I did not mention any of this to my friends. We spent another hour at the place and then drove back towards Mussoorie.

'I'm starving, let's find a place to eat,' Somesh urged. A little further up the road, we stumbled upon a quaint roadside shack.

'Maggi would be perfect right now!' I exclaimed.

Our arrival roused the man running the shack. His face brightened at the sight of potential customers. 'What can I get you folks? I've got Maggi, bun omelettes, grilled sandwiches and your choice of tea or coffee,' he offered.

'Five Maggis with vegetables and cheese, please,' I replied.

The man seemed genuinely pleased. I suspected business had been slow. With a friendly demeanour, he enquired about our origins. I explained that I was a local while my friends had travelled from Delhi.

'I lived in Delhi for two decades myself,' the man shared, 'before relocating to the hills.'

'Really?' Ashish chimed in. 'When did you come to Mussoorie?'

The man narrated that he'd been living in Mussoorie for five years, having left the capital after growing weary of the frenetic pace of city life. He also said that he had opened this modest shack to earn a simple living.

'By the way, I'm Sameer,' he said, extending his hand. We all took turns introducing ourselves.

Sameer, likely in his early fifties, was a tall, lean man with a cheerful disposition that shone through despite his weathered appearance. His long face, framed by greying hair, was characterized by a resolute chin that spoke volumes about his steadfast determination. His deep-set eyes indicated wisdom acquired through struggles and challenges he had encountered in life.

'Where are you headed?' He asked as he cut the vegetables for our Maggi. I told him that we had come for a random drive and had stumbled upon a charming spot a short distance away.

'We spent a few hours there, soaking in the breath-taking view of Doon Valley. Now we're heading back to Mussoorie.'

Sameer's demeanour abruptly shifted and his face became etched with alarm.

'Which place are you referring to? Was it the area with the old, abandoned buildings?'

His voice rose in urgency.

'Yes. That's the place,' I replied.

'That's the area of the Old Mines,' Sameer's voice

was thick with fear and concern. 'It's a haunted place. Why did you go there?'

'I've heard rumours about the Old Mines being one of the most haunted spots in Mussoorie,' I explained to Sameer, 'but I'd never actually been there before. I had no idea that any of those buildings were part of the Old Mines.'

Then I told him and my friends about my eerie experience inside the building.

'You are lucky that the malevolent spirits did not harm you,' Sameer said.

'I was the only person to reside there after the mines were shut down,' he whispered. 'I have seen and felt powerful evil there. I have witnessed and experienced the hauntings and narrowly escaped harm on several occasions.'

Upon our insistence, he shared some of his chilling experiences. After recounting a few tales, he paused and met our gaze. His eyes were filled with a haunting mystery.

'There are countless incidents like these that I've endured at the mine,' he continued. 'I had a very close call. It's been several years now, but I have never returned to that place. I urge you to stay away. That place is truly evil and dangerous.'

The concern in his voice was sincere.

Evening had descended upon us, and several hours slipped away as we sat captivated, sipping countless cups of tea while listening to Sameer recount the engrossing and chilling incidents that he had encountered.

We took his leave and hurried back to Mussoorie. Before departing, I exchanged numbers with him.

'We will be in touch,' I said.

After that I had several conversations with him over phone—every time I was curious to know more about the Old Mines.

Then, one morning, I received a call from him. His voice was weak and strained.

'I've been in an accident,' he managed to say. 'I have been admitted at the Civil Hospital. I need some medicine, clothes and other essentials. Could you please get them from the market? I'll reimburse you for the cost.'

I rushed to the hospital and found him in a dire state—deep cuts marred his forehead, his arm was encased in a plaster, and bruises covered his body.

'I have multiple fractures in my ribs and arm,' he whispered in a barely audible voice.

After getting a list of the items he needed, I went to the market, purchased everything and delivered them to him.

'I have no one else in this world,' Sameer confessed, tears of gratitude welling up in his eyes. 'I don't even have any friends. So I had to bother you, brother.'

I stayed in close contact with him throughout his week-long hospital stay. Once he started feeling better, he called me multiple times, insisting on repaying me for the items I had purchased despite my protests.

After a few months, I reached out to him to check on his health and learn more about the accident. Sameer told me that he had recently adopted a stray dog, and one morning he went missing.

'I was worried about Kalu. In this area dogs are often preyed upon by leopards,' he told me.

Sameer searched frantically for his pet all day before an acquaintance told him that he had seen Kalu on the road to the Old Mines. He did not want to go there again, but his concern for Kalu prompted him to go towards that side on his bike. Dusk was falling when he reached the building complex.

'Upon reaching there, I got off my bike and started walking ahead—calling out to Kalu. Suddenly, a foul stench hit me. It seemed to be emanating from my old room. Out of curiosity I peeped inside and saw a dark shadow on one of the walls,' Sameer's voice quivered as he recounted the event.

He immediately sensed that something sinister was afoot! Without delay, he ran back to his bike and sped back towards his shack.

'Even as I rode the bike, it felt like the stench was clinging to me,' Sameer recalled. 'I became convinced that the evil was pursuing me and that I was in mortal danger.'

He had barely made it to the main road when disaster struck—he and his bike veered off the road and plummeted into a gorge below.

'I didn't lose control of the bike. It felt like some unseen force lifted me and my bike and just hurled us off the road,' Sameer explained, emphasizing the unnatural nature of the accident.

He said that the malevolent forces had tried their best to end his life but he was fortunate to escape with some injuries.

'But the good thing was that when I went back to my shack after getting discharged from the hospital, Kalu was sitting outside waiting for me,' Sameer said, his eyes shining with happiness.

I am still in touch with Sameer and he still runs his shack, catering to both tourists and locals. I have never met a more contented person than him, who makes just enough to meet his requirements and is happy with his life!

As for the Old Mines, I have never dared to return to that place. Occasionally my curiosity prompts me to ask Sameer, 'Have you been to the mines again?' But he has vowed that no matter what, he will never go back there. I also pester him with questions regarding any other haunting that occurred at the mines. He says that so far he has not heard of any untoward incidents except a few people getting terrified and sick after visiting the place.

But he also tells me that the Old Mines have become quite popular on social media because of their spooky reputation, and attract lots of regular visitors. I am sure some of these foolhardy people have also felt the evil presence there. I just hope none of them come to any harm.

# The Whistling Intruder

In the 1960s, a middle-aged teacher named Miss L lived alone in a house on Camel's Back Road. In those days, the tortuous road was a terribly secluded place.

Residents on this road avoided leaving their homes once night fell, largely because of their deep-seated fears linked to the Parsi and Christian cemeteries on this road. The locals would whisper about the ghosts and restless spirits that haunted the road after sunset—with more enthusiasm than when they discussed the weather.

Many people claimed to have had ghastly experiences on Camel's Back Road. Some claimed to have seen spectral figures gliding through the trees, their faces obscured by ethereal mist. Others spoke of eerie sounds emanating from the cemeteries—mournful wails, chilling laughter and the distant clinking of chains.

As if this wasn't enough to instil a feeling of eeriness—especially on dark, whispery nights—Miss L's house overlooked the cemetery, further deepening the sense of wary loneliness that pervaded the surroundings.

It stood sentinel over the infamous road—a quaint, Victorian-style cottage surrounded by a vibrant garden. On clear mornings, it offered a panoramic view of the Himalaya, its snow-capped peaks shimmering in the sunlight. Below it lay the Camel's Back Cemetery, its tall deodar trees standing guard over the resting place of the town's departed.

Miss L lived a solitary life.

Each morning, she would rise before dawn and be out of the house by 6.30 a.m., bound for Hampton Court School where she taught. Her days were filled with the familiar rhythms of the classroom—chalk squeaking on a board, the murmur of students, the satisfying click of a pen. At lunchtime, she would often join her small circle of friends for a quiet meal, their conversations providing a welcome respite from the day's demands.

Once the school got over in the afternoon, she would head to the market—making occasional social calls at the homes of her handful of friends along the way—and shop for her daily needs at the Mall. Or she would go for solitary walks towards the Mussoorie Library. She found comfort in the familiar streets, known faces and quiet rhythm of life in the mountains.

Although a pucca socialite, the spinster preferred to finish her social sojourns and return to her house before sunset lest she run into any of Mussoorie's 'eternal residents'.

Her routine was as predictable as the mountain fog that rolled in each evening.

One evening Miss L got unusually late, and she ambled towards her house as dusk settled around her. As she hurried past the gate of the cemetery, she came upon a tall Englishman.

'Good evening, madam,' the stranger greeted politely, his voice imbued with a touch of old-world elegance.

Miss L responded with a nod as she scanned the man's attire—his dark suit was crisply tailored, there was a vibrant red tie around his neck, and the black hat on his head was worn with a slight tilt.

'Might you furnish me with the directions to Mall Road? Alas, I must confess, my last sojourn to Mussoorie was many years past, and I now perceive that the town has undergone a transformation of considerable extent.'

The stranger spoke in a manner most befitting the Victorian era. Miss L promptly guided him to Mall Road.

The stranger thanked her profusely and asked, 'Madam, from whence do you hail, and what business brings you upon this dark road?'

Miss L, an English teacher, was enjoying the conversation as she rarely heard such eloquent Victorian English.

'Oh, usually I am home by this time. But today I got delayed. My residence is just above,' she replied, gesturing towards her home perched atop the road.

The stranger's gaze followed her arm, his eyes widening in surprise as he took in the sight of the quaint Victorian cottage.

'Very well,' he said, extending his hand. 'I, Edwin Moore, am most delighted to make your acquaintance, madam.'

Miss L introduced herself in response and the duo struck up a conversation. He asked a lot of questions

about Mussoorie and about her. Ever the gracious conversationalist, Miss L responded with delight. She was taken by the courteous Englishman's old-world charm; after all, it was rare to find such a strikingly handsome bloke strolling aimlessly on her side of town!

It was all good, except for one little detail—something about his bloodshot eyes pinched her as strange. She would mention this to her friends later while she related the entire account. Despite finding it odd for someone so well-groomed, she let it slide, attributing it to lack of sleep. Engrossed in the conversation, Miss L had lost track of time and suddenly realized that it had become really dark. She quickly took leave of Edwin Moore and almost ran towards her house.

For many days Edwin lingered in her thoughts. While leaving for school in the morning or returning home in the evening, she would scan the surroundings, hoping to meet the enigmatic stranger again. One morning, as she stood outside her house staring at the cemetery and the desolate adjacent road, she thought longingly of him. 'Oh, he must have left by now,' she whispered, a deep sigh escaping her lips.

Miss L went on with her routine life. The handsome man she had met escaped her thoughts. But that is when things began to change dramatically—and not in a good way.

In the dead of night, as Miss L slept soundly, the light in her bedroom suddenly flickered on, jolting her awake.

'How did this turn on?' She wondered as her eyes

darted around the room searching for the signs of an intruder. 'Perhaps it hadn't been properly switched off, or the lever has become loose,' she mused, her gaze shifting to the brass toggle switch on the wall to her right. However, the following two nights, the light flickered on automatically again around the same time and left Miss L very unsettled. She caught hold of an electrician who examined the switch and even replaced it with a new one at her insistence.

The flickering stopped and Miss L breathed a sigh of relief.

'Just a stupid switch that had my heart fluttering,' she muttered.

After a few days, Miss L became engrossed in a romantic novel which kept her awake well past bedtime. Suddenly, she heard an eerie whistling sound emanating from outside her door. While whistling sounds are commonly associated with strong winds in the hills, this particular sound sent a shiver down her spine.

'Could it be the wind? But this whistling sound has a rhythmic, melodious quality, almost as if someone were humming a tune,' she pondered as she listened intently to the sound.

Suddenly, she realized that the tempo of the whistling had shifted, as if to a different tune.

Miss L was terrified. However, her mind didn't immediately turn to the supernatural. In that moment, she suspected it might be a stalker standing outside her door.

She promptly picked up her telephone and dialled the number of the police station. 'There is a stalker outside my door. I live alone and I am worried about my safety. Please send a constable immediately,' Miss L said to the person who received her call, her voice trembling slightly as she provided her address.

The whistling continued for several minutes until she heard the sound of several heavy footsteps approaching. Then it ceased immediately, and shortly thereafter, a loud knock sounded on her door. The scared woman confirmed the identity of her visitors before opening the door.

'Did you catch him?' She exclaimed.

'Who, madam?' One of the constables asked.

'The stalker! He was whistling outside my door just as I heard your footsteps climbing up the slope,' she said, her face etched with surprise.

'There seems to be only one way down, and no one passed us as we came up,' the other constable said.

Nonetheless, the policemen went around her house—examining her garden carefully—just to be certain. But there was no sign of anyone.

'Must have been the wind whistling in the trees, madam. There is no sign of anyone,' they reported with finality.

Miss L was adamant that the sound she heard had not been the wind, but an individual whistling a melody. But the officers, finding no corroborating evidence, politely told her that they would keep a watch over her house and left.

The next day, Miss L borrowed a hockey stick from the school's puzzled sports coach.

'Why on earth do you need a hockey stick?'

'Just to shoo away some pesky monkeys from my garden. I'll have it back to you in a few days,' she explained.

Back at home, Miss L placed the hockey stick beside her bed.

'If he dares to break in, I'll give him a thrashing he won't forget.'

Things remained quiet for a few days, until—one night—the eerie whistling resumed. Initially gripped by intense fear, Miss L managed to gather some courage and yelled, 'Go away! Or I'll shoot you with my pistol.'

After a few moments the whistling stopped. Miss L thought that the stalker had been frightened by her threat. Next day, she boasted of her bravery to all her colleagues at the school. But that night the whistling resumed again.

Miss L's emotions were a mixture of fury and dread. She yelled at the intruder from the safety of her room, commanding him to leave her grounds and threatening to shoot him!

Taunting her defiance, the eerie whistling continued.

Miss L dialled the number of the police again. But like before, just as the sound of heavy boots was heard on the walkway to her house, the eerie whistling abruptly ceased.

'Ma'am, we've scoured the area. There is no one

around,' declared the constable, his voice carrying a bit of impatience.

Miss L insisted, 'It stopped just as your footsteps sounded on the walkway, like it knew you were coming!'

The officers exchanged glances with barely concealed amusement, as if they already knew that they would find nothing. They seemed to believe that Miss L's nightly visitor was nothing more than the whispering wind or perhaps a figment of her imagination.

The next morning, Miss L opened the door of her house to find a bunch of daisies lying at her doorstep. She realized that this was the work of the stalker. Frustrated and angry, she sent the daisies scattering with a swift kick. That night, the whistling was followed by a gentle knock on her door. Her voice trembled with fear and defiance as she yelled, 'Go away! Go away! I am calling the police.'

A sudden realization struck her—she hadn't drawn the curtain of the window by the door. Her heart pounded as she noticed a tall, ominous shadow stretched across the glass, a chilling silhouette against the dim light. The figure was unmistakably human, crowned with what seemed to be the brim of a hat; its motionless shadow, stark against the glass, lurked just outside her door— watching and waiting. A surge of panic flooded Miss L and she rushed to pull the curtain closed, desperate to shut out the terrifying presence.

Then—shuddering with fear—Miss L slumped into the corner, clutching the hockey stick tightly in her hands. Her soft, helpless sobs barely disturbed the heavy silence that followed the eerie whistling and ominous knocks.

Mercifully, nothing more happened that night.

Miss L was gripped by a deep-seated terror. Yet, she knew calling the police would be futile. Just like before, the mysterious intruder would vanish right as the police arrived. Anger surged through her fear. 'I'll meet the inspector first thing tomorrow. This has to end!' She vowed silently.

The following morning, Miss L found another bunch of daisies lying at her doorstep—an unnerving reminder of the stalker's relentless pursuit. In a surge of defiance and disgust, she stomped on the flowers, grinding them into the pavement with her heel.

As she stepped outside her house and walked to the edge of her garden, she noticed that a vast expanse of daisies bloomed in the cemetery below, their white petals forming a stark contrast against the sombre backdrop.

'So, the damned criminal is fetching these daisies from the cemetery,' she muttered. 'But *who* is he and *why* is he stalking me?'

That afternoon, after school concluded, Miss L made her way to the police station. There she was met by Inspector Sharma, a man known for his gentle demeanour and patient ear. He listened attentively as Miss L, visibly shaken and distressed, recounted the events that had transpired.

'Madam, I am well aware of your complaints. Acting on them, we sent constables to your house on multiple occasions. But they found neither an intruder nor any evidence suggesting one was there,' Inspector Sharma explained, his voice laced with a mix of sympathy and professional concern.

'But I am not lying, inspector. There is definitely an intruder stalking me and he is smart enough to disappear before your constables can spot him,' Miss L pleaded.

Determined to convince Inspector Sharma of the gravity of her situation, Miss L proceeded to narrate each incident in vivid detail. She told him about the unsettling whistling and the ominous knocks at her door. She described the silhouette she had seen outside her window and finally the daisies left on her doorstep.

The kindly inspector was touched by the palpable fear in Miss L's eyes. 'Madam,' he said in a reassuring voice, 'I understand your fear. I will send a team of constables to your house every night until this scoundrel is caught. They'll be discreet, in plain clothes, and with your consent, will stay inside your house to remain unseen. As soon as the intruder arrives, they will nab him.'

With a newfound sense of hope, Miss L stepped out of the police station. Noticing the fading daylight, she quickened her pace—passing by the familiar Cambridge Book Depot before turning onto Lavender Lane that led to Camel's Back Road—and eventually resorted to a near-run, eager to reach the safety of her home before darkness fell. As she approached the cemetery gate, her heart skipped a beat; silhouetted against the fading light, just outside the entrance of the cemetery, stood a man.

As Miss L apprehensively took a few steps closer,

her fear turned to relief. 'Oh, Mr Edwin! You startled me!' she exclaimed, recognizing the familiar face of the Englishman.

'How do you fare this evening, madam?' Edwin greeted her in his distinct Victorian accent.

'I am very well, Mr Edwin. I looked out for you for many days to no avail. I thought you had left Mussoorie.'

'Nay, my lady, I have been here throughout,' Edwin replied suavely.

'Then why didn't you come to call upon me at my home?'

'Oh, but my lady, I did indeed call upon your residence on numerous occasions; however, you did not open the door despite my entreaties,' Edwin lamented. 'I even brought you daisies, plucked from near my final resting place in the cemetery, yet you trampled them underfoot with disdain.'

As he spoke, his face contorted into a ghastly visage. His eyes blazed with an unearthly gleam, adding a chilling edge to each word.

Miss L felt a wave of terror wash over her and the ground seemed to shift beneath her feet. She stood paralyzed with shock as a sinister grin spread across the man's face. He reached out to grab her, his long and bony fingers resembling the talons of a nocturnal predator.

Somehow, Miss L was able to come out of her reverie.

'Gh-ghost! *Ghost!* Help me!'

Her scream pierced the eerie silence. Before the spectral fingers could reach her, she whirled around and fled. Fuelled by sheer terror, she ran faster than she ever had, her heart pounding like a drum; she didn't pause, didn't slow, didn't dare look back.

She ran until she had scaled the steep Lavender Lane—her lungs burning and her legs screaming in protest! She ran until she reached the familiar bustle of Mall Road—a wave of relief washing over her as she stumbled into the crowd...

That night, Miss L stayed with the nuns at the school. The next morning, she went back to her house accompanied by a few teachers, packed her bags and promptly left—never to return again.

The tale of Edwin Moore and his spectral connection to Miss L continues to captivate the residents of Mussoorie, fuelling endless speculation. Many have even attempted to locate Edwin Moore's grave, but without success. Perhaps his resting place is unmarked or the headstone has been damaged over time.

Nowadays, residents living close to the cemetery frequently walk past its gate at night. Tourists are often seen indulging in night-time revelry near it. There have been no reports of anyone encountering the ghostly English gentleman. Even I have moved around the Camel's Back at late hours—sometimes well past midnight and often alone—but am yet to meet any Englishman.

Why did the Englishman's spirit haunt Miss L? Why has the spirit not appeared to anyone else? Is he really buried in the Camel's Back Cemetery?

If it's any consolation, this isn't the first—and surely

won't be the last—mystery of Mussoorie whose answer has been buried in its dense forests, or carried away by the blanket of fog.

∞

# Pari Tibba

A small hill behind the students' hostel of Woodstock School is perhaps the most mysterious place in Mussoorie. Local residents—seniors and youngsters alike—swear on God that *paris*, or fairies, visit this hill and have thus christened it as 'Pari Tibba'.

This hill has a large, flat ground at the top, surprisingly devoid of vegetation despite being enveloped by dense forest on all sides. The soil at the hilltop exhibits a distinct black, charred appearance. Local folklores attribute the lack of vegetation and blackened soil to frequent lightning strikes.

The tales and legends woven around Pari Tibba are nothing short of extraordinary, surpassing even the most bizarre paranormal stories recounted in this book. These narratives—passed down through generations—speak of encounters with ethereal beings, adding another layer of mystique to this already captivating hill.

Our story begins almost two centuries ago—in the early nineteenth century—when the township of Mussoorie was in its formative years. In the 1830s, Captain Conor—a British army officer stationed at Dehradun, and a frequent visitor to Mussoorie—wanted to build

a summer home here to escape the scorching heat of the plains.

He was scouting around the town looking for a scenic location away from habitation, when he chanced upon Pari Tibba. This isolated hill seemed perfect for his home—nestled among verdant oak forests, offering a breath-taking view, and conveniently located close to a perennial stream.

Captain Conor found that the hill belonged to a neighbouring village, but the villagers refused to sell it. 'This is holy land, inhabited by paris who protect us. We will not sell this land,' the village headman said. He gestured towards an unusual and seemingly abstract cluster of stones at one end of the hilltop—the stones were adorned with a red *tika* while dried flowers were strewn about the place.

'This is the temple of the paris where they descend from the heavens on auspicious nights,' the headman explained. 'We also offer prayers here to appease them.'

An infuriated Conor declared that he would construct his house on that very hill. The village headman pleaded with him, cautioning him of divine retribution if the sanctity of the place was disturbed. Arrogant and dismissive, the Englishman merely scoffed at the headman's warning and started construction on Pari Tibba.

The sight of construction work on the hill filled the villagers' hearts with dread—they feared that the paris would unleash their fury on everyone for defiling their holy land.

Within a few months, the walls had risen defiantly, but then something strange began to happen. Workers found that the stone walls had started to crumble.

'Saheb, every morning we find that a wall has collapsed. These are strong stone walls, we are not able to understand why they are crumbling. There is something wrong!' The foreman urgently communicated to Conor in Dehradun, who promptly rushed to Mussoorie and arrived at Pari Tibba. Addressing the workers in a stern tone, he declared, 'You fools! You are not constructing the walls properly.'

Conor took a furlough and set up a camp there. 'Now I will personally monitor the construction work,' he announced.

The construction resumed under Conor's watchful eye. Although the incidents of collapsing walls declined, occasional setbacks persisted. Despite the challenges, Conor persevered and successfully completed the wall construction. Feeling pleased with himself, Conor directed the workers to fell the rhododendron trees growing around Pari Tibba for the roof construction. He himself returned to his army base at Dehradun. In the next few weeks, a significant number of trees surrounding Pari Tibba were felled and transported to the construction site.

It was late June and monsoon arrived with a vengeance. Torrential rains poured down for three days, wreaking havoc on the neighbouring villages. Several houses were destroyed and there was extensive damage to the farms. Thankfully, no lives were lost.

Fear gripped the villagers. 'This is the wrath of the paris. They are punishing us for the desecration of their holy grounds by the *gora*!' They whispered.

Finally, the rains subsided and the villagers heaved a collective sigh of relief. 'We must meet the gora saheb and stop his house construction,' they decided in a meeting.

But before the villagers could act, a powerful thunderstorm struck that night. The following morning, news spread that Conor's house had been struck by lightning, resulting in its complete destruction.

This news spread like wildfire, shrouding the hill in further fear and mystery. People claimed that it was the 'devil's handiwork'! Many fervently believed that witches resided at Pari Tibba. In fact, believing that the lightning was the handiwork of witches, the Europeans christened it as the 'Witch's Hill' and avoided approaching it. Apart from occasional picnic trips during the day, no one ventured there after dark.

For several decades thereafter, no other significant occurrences at Pari Tibba came to light, although the villagers continued to be startled by frequent lightning strikes that punctuated the hill.

In 1896, Colonel Montgomery, a decorated army officer, relocated to the serene Landour cantonment following his retirement. He settled in a large mansion near Lal Tibba with his wife and daughter.

Enjoying his retirement, the colonel spent long hours drinking and gambling at the then famous Himalaya Club. He would leave his house after lunch and return around midnight, much to the chagrin of his wife Ruth.

The colonel's daughter, Emily, was a picture of elegance and charm. Her eyes, radiant and captivating, rivalled the brilliance of the jewels that adorned her delicate neck. Her melodious laughter carried joyously on the wind and her spirit shone with the warmth of the rising sun.

Although Emily kept to herself and had no close companions, she was the object of admiration for every young officer at the Landour Cantonment. Their gazes invariably followed her, filled with an unspoken longing. Emily met Lieutenant James Bernard at an official function at the cantonment. The young man captured Emily's heart with his charming smile and gentle demeanour. Their love story blossomed amidst the tall deodars of Landour, their bond deepening with each passing day.

Meanwhile, unknown to the family, Colonel Montgomery was losing substantial sums of money on gambling—far exceeding what his army pension could cover. He became deeply ensnared in debt, which drove him to gamble more recklessly in a desperate attempt to recover his losses and settle his debts.

Jacob, a Jewish merchant from Saharanpur, who also owned a store in Mussoorie, had been generously lending money to the colonel. One fateful night, the colonel suffered a devastating loss of 1,000 rupees at the gambling table. Desperate, he approached Jacob, seeking additional funds to repay his debts.

'Colonel,' Jacob began, his eyes gleaming with a

calculating glint, 'you already owe me 2,000 rupees. Now you are asking for an additional thousand. I require some form of surety, some collateral.'

'But what can I possibly offer you? I have nothing of value!' The colonel exclaimed in desperation.

'Well then,' the shrewd merchant replied, 'why don't you mortgage your fine mansion to me? Once you repay your debt in full, I shall release the mortgage.'

The colonel reluctantly agreed and paid off his debt with the money he received from the Shylock. But he refused to learn from his follies and continued gambling, adding on to his mounting debts.

One evening, as the colonel approached Jacob seeking yet another loan, the moneylender firmly refused. 'I have already extended you considerable credit, and you haven't even managed to pay the interest,' Jacob declared. 'I am taking possession of your house. You have two days to vacate the premises.'

The colonel was stunned. He pleaded endlessly with Jacob, who remained unmoved. So he trudged back to his home, blaming his gambling addiction for his dire state. He narrated the entire incident to Ruth, who was enraged. But having no other option, she reluctantly began preparations to vacate their cherished home.

On the appointed day, Jacob arrived at the colonel's residence to claim ownership of the property. He was met with a scene of frantic activity. The colonel, Ruth and Emily were hurriedly packing their belongings, their faces etched with despair.

Seeing Jacob, the colonel made a desperate attempt to persuade the moneylender to give them some time to repay the debt.

'Please, Jacob, don't take away my home. I swear I will repay every penny I owe,' he pleaded.

Meanwhile, Jacob harboured dark designs on Emily. He had been utterly enamoured by the young girl's beauty and, despite being much older than the girl, he desired her as his wife.

'Colonel, I am a compassionate man,' he said with a sly grin. 'If you were to offer me something of substantial value, I would be willing to forgive your debt entirely and allow you to keep your house.'

'What can I give you?' the colonel asked, his voice hopeful.

'Emily,' the sly moneylender said, leaving the colonel, Ruth and Emily stunned.

The colonel and Ruth flatly refused. However, Emily—her eyes brimming with tears—reluctantly agreed. Her decision was driven by her love for her parents and a desperate desire to save their home.

Thus, Emily and Jacob were married in a quiet ceremony at St. Paul's Church, and shortly thereafter, they departed for Saharanpur. James was devastated, but before Emily left, she managed to meet him and explain the dire circumstances that prompted this decision. James, though heartbroken, managed a sad smile and said, 'Emily, I understand you had no other choice. But remember, I will always be there for you, whenever you need me.'

Emily found herself trapped in a loveless marriage. Although Jacob treated her with kindness and respect, she could never find happiness in his company. Emily's once vibrant spirit gradually faded and her cheerful laughter became a distant memory.

Meanwhile, James was transferred to the Meerut cantonment. Being a charming young man, he received numerous proposals for marriage, but was unable to erase the memory of Emily from his heart.

As time wore on, weakened by years of emotional turmoil, Emily became frail and fell ill. Yearning to spend some time at her home, she expressed her desire to Jacob. Hoping that the gentle climate, familiar surroundings and the loving care of her mother might aid in her recovery, he promptly sent Emily to Landour.

As Emily arrived in Landour and rode through the narrow streets, her thoughts drifted back to the happy days of her youth. She remembered the stolen glances with James, the whispered promises of eternal love, and the towering deodars that had silently witnessed their blossoming romance.

Meanwhile, fate was weaving its magic once again. James, now a captain, was also in Landour on an extended leave. One evening, while strolling through Sister's Bazaar, he unexpectedly crossed paths with Emily, who was standing outside a shop with her mother. As their eyes met, time seemed to stand still. They gazed at each other, their hearts overflowing with emotions that had been buried for years.

Cupid struck again! Emily and James began meeting regularly, their rekindled romance becoming the talk of the town. Emily's parents, still burdened by the guilt of sacrificing their daughter's happiness, did not seem to object. Meanwhile, James's presence acted as a balm to Emily's weary soul, and her health began to improve noticeably.

The news of their romance reached Jacob, who became mad with rage. Planning to punish the couple, he gathered his men and some goons, and left for Mussoorie. As they reached Jharipani, James somehow caught wind of their arrival. He rushed to Emily's home to warn her of the imminent danger, and the couple made the bold decision to elope. Knowing that Jacob and his men were coming up via the Jharipani-Barlowgunj route, James and Emily chose the treacherous goat tracks that descended into the ravine below Woodstock School and continued on to Dehradun.

It was already late evening when the couple embarked on their perilous journey. They wanted to reach the Ringal stream and follow its course downstream until they reached the safety of Rajpur.

As Emily and James cautiously made their way downhill, Jacob and his men arrived in Landour. From the ridge, Jacob spotted the fleeing couple. With a roar of fury, he and his men gave chase, quickly descending the same path.

James—hearing the rustling of bushes and heavy footsteps behind them—realized they were being pursued. He grasped Emily's hand and urged her across the Ringal stream and up the steep slope towards Pari Tibba. Perhaps his plan was to cross the hill and reach Chamasari village, where they could seek shelter.

Jacob, recounting the pursuit later, claimed to have seen the couple ascend the slope of Pari Tibba. 'They were within our sights,' he said, 'but suddenly, such a torrential downpour began that we were unable to proceed any further.'

It is said that the relentless downpour prevented the couple from crossing Pari Tibba, compelling them to seek refuge within the crumbling remnants of Conor's ill-fated house. The rain and thunderstorm raged throughout the night. When Jacob and his men finally reached Pari Tibba the following morning, they were met with a chilling sight. Within the ruins lay the charred bodies of Emily and James, locked in a final, eternal embrace.

They are said to have been buried at Pari Tibba.

The truth of what transpired at Pari Tibba on that fateful night remains shrouded in mystery, buried forever with Emily and James. Perhaps they encountered the paris, perhaps even communicated with them. No one could say for certain.

Did the paris actually take their lives, or was it merely a tragic coincidence that lightning struck the very spot where the couple had sought refuge?

But the villagers were sure this was no coincidence. 'They had somehow angered the paris,' the villagers believed. They recounted that on that fateful night, a violent thunderstorm had unleashed its fury upon the hill. The thunder was deafening and the lightning relentless—striking Pari Tibba repeatedly.

'There was an ominous feeling in the air,' they said, their voices hushed with reverence. 'Perhaps it was the night the paris chose to descend. Enraged to find the couple trespassing on their sacred ground, they unleashed their wrath, and the couple was struck down by lightning.' This was the belief that took root among the villagers, further solidifying the legend of Pari Tibba.

In the absence of any eyewitness, what transpired at Pari Tibba with Conor or with Emily and James remains mere speculation—met with a mix of belief and scepticism. The sceptics firmly maintained that these two incidents were nothing more than unfortunate coincidences.

But the perception changed when Mr Sunder Rana emerged with a firsthand account of his unsettling encounter at Pari Tibba in the early 1960s. A childhood friend of my father, he once shared this chilling tale with me, leaving an indelible mark on my memory.

Mr Rana, who lived in Barlowgunj, was an avid hunter accustomed to pursuing jungle fowls and bush quails that thrived in the forests near Barlowgunj and Jharipani. During the summer, two of his friends from Dehradun visited him, drawn by the promise of a hunting expedition.

'There's plenty of small game around,' Mr Rana assured them, 'we'll have a grand time.'

But his friends craved the thrill of tracking and bagging larger, more elusive preys. 'We're not interested in mere birds,' they determinedly declared. 'We're after something more substantial—a *ghoral* or a deer, at the very least.'

So off they went, taking the goat path up to Mossy Falls, then descending to the Ringal stream and moving northwards along it. 'This area is densely forested, home to ghoral and deer,' Mr Rana remarked, his voice tinged with anticipation. 'But be careful, as bears also roam these woods.'

As the trio moved up the stream, they sighted ghorals and also a couple of deer. However, before they could raise their guns and take aim, the elusive animals vanished into the dense undergrowth.

'This is incredibly frustrating,' Manish grumbled. 'We've been at it for two hours, and we haven't managed to get even a single shot at anything.'

Mr Rana, sensing his friends' disappointment, felt a pang of guilt. 'Don't be disheartened,' he encouraged, 'there's plenty of game to be found in these woods. Let's press on a bit further and keep our guns ready.'

It was late afternoon and in their zeal for game, the trio had walked several kilometres along the stream, passing the students' hostel of Woodstock School perched on a hill above the stream.

Exhausted and hungry, they found a clearing and sat down to rest and consume the packed lunch that they were carrying.

Mr Rana, sensing the potential blame for a failed hunting trip, was determined to redeem himself. Eager to find some game for his friends, he suggested, 'There's a dense forest just beyond. Let's try our luck there. We're sure to find something.'

The trio walked ahead, venturing deeper into the dense forest. They meandered away from the stream, ascending the slopes to their right. But it seemed as if the animals had been forewarned of their arrival—not a ghoral or deer was to be seen. Only a few jungle fowls fluttered nervously in the undergrowth.

'Let's bag a few of them,' Manish urged. 'Better than going home empty handed.' He quickly raised his gun and shot a few of the birds.

The sunlight had begun to fade and the visibility was declining—especially underneath the thick canopy of the dense oak forest. 'We must head back before it gets dark,' Mr Rana said urgently.

They promptly turned back, walking with rapid steps as they attempted to reach the familiar stream that would help them navigate their way back. They had walked for about half an hour but could not reach the stream. Daylight had faded considerably by then, and the forest floor was plunged into an eerie gloom. Since this was intended to be a day trip, the trio had not brought any flashlights.

'It is difficult to make out our surroundings. Where is the darned stream, Rana?' Gopal shouted, his voice filled with panic. Mr Rana, who was leading the way, was at a loss for words. He remained silent and increased his pace.

Night fell soon and the would-be hunters could barely see a few feet ahead of them.

'We are lost, friends,' Mr Rana declared, his voice heavy with resignation.

Gopal and Manish were enraged. It was fortunate that Mr Rana could not clearly discern the extent of fury on their faces in the dim light.

'I am sorry, guys, I got you into this!' Mr Rana said apologetically. 'No point wandering about in the dark; let's find a clearing and settle down for the night.'

As they moved forward, straining their eyes in the darkness, they could just discern the faint outline of a low hilltop silhouetted against the night sky.

'Let's head there,' Manish suggested, pointing towards the hill. 'It might help us get our bearings and offer a safer place to rest.' The others agreed and they began the slow, careful climb to the summit.

Upon reaching the top, they were surprised to find a large, flat area—almost the size of a football field. It was devoid of any vegetation, creating an eerie, barren landscape under the moonlight. They could make out a strange collection of stones at one end of the flat, while at the other end stood a crumbling ruin.

'Let's camp in the ruins—they will provide some shelter from rain and winds,' Mr Rana suggested and the three of them headed towards them.

The trio had unwittingly ventured into the infamous

Pari Tibba and were approaching the ruins of Conor's house—the very place where Emily and James had met their tragic end. Had they known this, they would have fled the god-forsaken place as fast as their legs could carry them!

Instead, the tired and dejected hunters sprawled on the ground—bathed in the soft glow of the full moon—and gazed at the starry sky, until Manish reminded them of the need to prepare dinner. He proudly retrieved two fowls from the rucksack and placed them on the ground.

'We need to clean them and cook them over a fire,' he said. 'It's a pity that we don't have any spices to flavour them.'

Feeling famished after the day's exertion, they quickly got to work. Mr Rana and Manish set off in search of dried wood on the slopes surrounding the summit, while Gopal took out his hunting knife to clean and prepare the birds. Gathering some stones lying in the ruins, they arranged a makeshift fire pit outside the ruins and began roasting the meat.

'Let me roast the fowls,' Manish offered. The crackling of the fire broke the silence as the trio gazed intently at the roasting meat, their hunger growing with each passing moment. Soon, the tantalizing aroma of cooked meat filled the air.

'This delightful aroma is making by stomach rumble,' Gopal quipped, eliciting chuckles from the others.

The night was still, save for the occasional rustle of leaves and the distant hoot of an owl. Suddenly, a loud

clap of thunder shattered the tranquillity of the night.
The moon disappeared behind a veil of dark clouds, and
a powerful gust of wind swept across the hilltop.

Within minutes, a heavy downpour began. Before
they could even react, the fire was extinguished and their
precious meat was soaked. They scrambled for cover
inside the ruins, and to their surprise, the rain ceased
as abruptly as it had begun. The clouds parted and the
moon emerged from behind its veil, casting its pale glow
over the hilltop.

The trio stood dumbfounded, their faces etched with
a mixture of surprise and fear.

'What was that?'

Their confused voices echoed in the sudden silence.

'Our dinner is ruined and we will have to sleep on
empty stomachs,' Mr Rana lamented as he dejectedly
slumped upon a damp stone.

Once more, an eerie silence descended upon the
hilltop, broken only by the soft rustle of leaves in the
breeze and the distant calls of nocturnal creatures. The
air grew heavy with an unsettling stillness and a palpable
sense of unease prickled their skin.

From the corner of his eyes, Mr Rana noticed a faint
shimmering light emanating from the cluster of stones
to his right. It pulsed and throbbed, growing brighter
with each passing moment. A cold sweat beaded on his
forehead as he turned to face the light. He watched
it, transfixed. Manish and Gopal followed the line of
his sight and their gazes were also captured by the

inexplicable glow emanating from the stones.

Suddenly, five figures emerged from the light—as if from a shimmering portal connected with another dimension. As the figures stepped forward, the light behind them dimmed until it was just a faint glow. The three men stood transfixed, jaws agape and eyes wide. The sight of figures materializing from thin air sent shockwaves through their senses.

The figures were actually women of a slender and graceful build. Each was dressed in a flowing robe that seemed to shimmer and change colours. They had delicate features, with large, expressive eyes that sparkled like magnificent diamonds. Their skin shone with a radiant glow, like moonlight captured in human form. They seemed to defy gravity, their feet not touching the ground but hovering in the air.

'They are paris!' Mr Rana realized. 'Oh God, we have reached Pari Tibba!'

A wave of dread passed over him

He had heard about this being the sacred ground of the paris and also about occurrences in the past when they harmed those who had trespassed. As Mr Rana realized the danger they were in, his heart thundered in his chest, each beat like a loud drum beat in the still night. Fear constricted his throat, stealing his breath and leaving him gasping for air.

Before he could react, the pari in the middle glided forward. Her eyes burned with otherworldly rage and her face was twisted in grotesque fury. She shouted in an arcane language and her voice boomed across the valley, echoing off the surrounding hills. Although neither Mr Rana nor his companions understood what she was saying, he was convinced that their actions had angered the paris.

Manish and Gopal exchanged terrified glances, pale-faced and trembling. Terror seized Mr Rana and he turned and ran like a madman, his legs pumping with desperate urgency. Manish and Gopal were right behind him.

Another deafening thunderclap boomed, followed by a blinding flash of lightning. The ground shook violently beneath their feet and they realized with horror that the lightning had struck perilously close.

'They w-w-want to k-k-kill us!' Manish shouted in panic as he sprinted behind Mr Rana and Gopal, his voice breaking with each ragged gasp of air.

After crossing the flat summit, they plunged downhill into the dense forest. They stumbled forward blindly in the dark—branches scraping their faces and hands, tearing at their clothes—as their lungs burned with exertion. Yet, fear propelled them onward and none dared to stop.

After running for what seemed like an eternity—just as their lungs were about to burst and their legs were on the verge of giving out—the trio spotted lights glimmering a short distance ahead.

'That's the village,' Mr Rana gasped, his voice filled with renewed hope. 'Come on. We'll be safe there!' He declared, urging his companions onward.

The sight of the lights gave them a renewed burst of energy. They pushed forward, driven by the promise of safety. The fear that had gripped their hearts seemed to loosen its icy grasp, replaced by a flicker of hope.

Mr Rana was the first to reach the small village. He collapsed at the door of the nearest house, his chest heaving and mind reeling from the encounter.

His companions soon joined him, and they frantically banged on the door of the house.

'Help! HELP!' Manish and Gopal shouted, their voices hoarse with desperation.

Hearing their clamour, the owner of the house, along with several people from neighbouring houses, emerged to investigate the commotion.

Mr Rana, utterly exhausted and terrified, could not utter a word. After a short pause Manish croaked, '*Bhoot...*' his voice filled with terror.

'Where? What happened?' The villagers asked as they helped the three men to their feet and took them to the house of Shambhu, the village headman. An elderly man of medium height and stout build, Shambhu had a kind and calm demeanour. He placed a comforting hand on Mr Rana's shoulder and invited the three friends inside his house.

After catching their breath and regaining some composure, the shaken men slowly narrated their terrifying experience at Pari Tibba. The villagers grouped around, listening intently.

'The Pari Tibba is sacred ground for the paris,' Shambhu explained, his voice grave. 'They frequent the area, especially on full-moon nights. You not only trespassed on their land but also defiled it by cooking meat there.'

He paused, his gaze sweeping over the three men. 'That lightning strike was meant to kill you all. You are incredibly fortunate to have escaped just in time.'

Mr Rana nodded, his face pale. 'We're lucky to be alive,' he murmured, 'but will the paris be able to harm us now?'

'Don't worry,' the headman assured him. 'You are out of harm's way now. The paris are generally benevolent beings unless provoked. They won't harm you anymore.'

'Baba, how do you know so much about the paris?' Gopal asked.

A prolonged silence followed. The headman seemed hesitant to answer, a flicker of unease crossing his features. He took a deep breath, as if preparing to divulge a closely guarded secret.

'Son, this legend goes back nearly two centuries and has been passed down through our family over generations,' he said, his gaze distant and lost, as if peering across the mists of time.

Shambhu recounted the tale of one of his ancestors, the erstwhile village headman—a god-fearing and pious man—who once decided to allow villagers to take up cultivation on the barren land atop Pari Tibba.

'The land belonged to the village,' Shambhu

explained. 'My ancestor believed it had the potential to be transformed into farmland, which would greatly benefit everyone.'

He said that on the same night that this decision was taken in a village meeting, his ancestor had a vivid dream. In it, he saw many paris who told him that the hill's summit was their sacred ground and must remain undisturbed by human activity.

'They summoned him to come alone to the summit on the approaching full-moon night to meet them,' Shambhu continued, his voice hushed.

'My ancestor was both confused and disturbed by this dream. He sought counsel from the village *pandit*, who told him that there was no harm in going to the hilltop on a full-moon night.'

So, his ancestor went to the summit as instructed in his dream. 'He waited for several hours and finally the stones lit up and the paris appeared—just as you have experienced. They told my ancestor that he must protect their sacred land, and in return, they would bless and protect the village. From that day forward, everyone in the village began calling the hill Pari Tibba.'

Shambhu explained that the unusual collection of stones at the summit was, in fact, a temple for the paris.

'The plans to cultivate the summit were immediately abandoned by my ancestor,' Shambhu said. 'Since then, our village has refrained from any activity on Pari Tibba— we don't even venture there after sunset. In return, the paris bless us with bountiful harvests every year, and our village has remained untouched by calamities like landslides and cloudbursts.'

He then shared the story of Conor and his ill-fated decision to build a house on the hilltop.

'That was the only year our village experienced a devastating cloudburst, causing damage to our fields and homes.'

Shambhu told the three visitors to have some dinner and rest. 'In the morning, my people will show you the way back to Barlowgunj.'

After sharing his harrowing tale, Mr Rana confided in me that though he and his friends had escaped unharmed, the memory of that encounter haunted them forever. He vowed never to return to that part of the forest again.

But I ended up visiting Pari Tibba a few years ago—curiosity getting the better of me! Unable to muster the courage to go there at night, I ventured there in the afternoon.

I found the hilltop to be exactly as described—barren and devoid of trees. There were some old ruins, and at one end, there was a peculiar collection of stones. It appeared as though someone had applied a red tika to these stones. Dried flowers lay scattered around them.

'This is an ancient temple where the paris come and pray,' said Sawan, who lived nearby and had accompanied me to Pari Tibba.

'And what about the tika and flowers—were they also offered by the paris?' I enquired.

'No no,' he exclaimed. 'Sometimes residents of Dhobighat and nearby villages come here to pray in these temples. These must have been left by them.'

Apart from the old ruins, it seemed that an attempt had been made recently to construct a building towards the southern end of the hilltop.

'About 10 years ago, a businessman from Delhi attempted to build a resort here. But it was never completed. At night the paris would demolish the walls, until finally the businessman gave up,' Sawan told me.

'What rubbish! Must be some locals who do not want any construction here,' I mocked in an attempt to provoke Sawan.

'Sir, you people never seem to understand! The owner of this place also thought the same and deployed several guards to catch the culprit, but a few hours past midnight all the guards would fall asleep, and in the morning the walls would be razed to the ground,' Sawan retorted, sounding a bit offended.

I spoke to several residents, particularly those living in Dhobighat nearby. I was told that no one visited the hill after sunset as paris are supposed to come there.

For me, Pari Tibba, or the Burnt Hill, remains the most mysterious place in the entire Mussoorie and Landour landscape! It is a place where the veil between the natural and supernatural seems palpably thin.

∽

# Hooves at Midnight

M y friend Vipin—resident of a remote hill village—had come to Mussoorie in the early 1990s in search of a job. He found employment as a manager in a small hotel until it was sold by the owners. He was job hunting when he came to know about a vacancy in Richmond Hotel (name changed).

'It was late March, I was looking for work when I came to know that all of a sudden most of the staff of Richmond Hotel had left. Seeing this as a great opportunity, I visited the hotel and was promptly appointed as the manager,' Vipin said.

He asked the management about the reason for the collective exodus of the earlier staff.

'Oh, they were a bad lot! They were caught hosting a noisy liquor party in duty hours. Shocked and frustrated, we confronted them about their unprofessional behaviour and they abruptly quit,' was the response.

Satisfied with the reply, Vipin thought no more about this matter and started working zealously at his new job.

'I was desperate for work and they were paying well. The owners stayed in Delhi but visited often, while we kept in regular contact through telephone.'

The Richmond Hotel was located near Mall Road and was built in the late 1980s. It was an impressive three-storeyed building with rooms that offered sweeping views of the Doon valley. The building also had a large basement where the kitchen and employee quarters were located. Nestled in a depression below the road, the hotel sat adjacent to a rivulet (locally called a *khala*). This rivulet, which flowed only during the monsoons, traced the boundary of the hotel before plunging into a deep gorge below. Entry to the hotel was through a small bridge built across the rivulet.

'Richmond Hotel was constructed by a few senior Congress leaders of the eighties and nineties. While it catered to a limited number of tourists, the primary purpose of this hotel was to oblige and entertain politicians, bureaucrats and rich businessmen,' Vipin said.

He revealed the names of several politicians, bureaucrats, lawyers and businessmen who often visited the hotel. I was surprised by the long list of bigwigs of that era, although I cannot reveal these names to you for obvious reasons.

After taking up his new job, the biggest challenge for Vipin was to recruit new staff in place of those who had quit.

'I was surprised that workers from Mussoorie were reluctant to join Richmond Hotel despite the higher wages. A few that turned up for interviews did not return. Finally, I had to persuade many of my friends from the village to join.'

By mid-April all the recruitments were complete. Apart from Vipin, there was an assistant manager, several people for housekeeping and room service, a chef and his few helpers.

'I think there were 10 to 12 staff members. All of them lived in small, double-sharing rooms in the basement, while I—being the manager—had a larger room for myself on the same floor. It was a challenging period, particularly with the new staff, many of whom did not have much experience in the hospitality industry. But all of us worked hard and we were able to manage,' Vipin recalled.

Things were normal for the first few months.

'We worked tirelessly day and night, and by the time we finished our duties, we were exhausted and succumbed to deep slumber.'

After the onset of monsoon in July, the number of visitors declined and they got some respite from work.

'We all were able to finish the work early and get more hours of sleep,' he said.

But once the hotel was vacant, weird things started happening. Two staff members who slept in a room at the edge of the hotel—adjoining the rivulet—reported their room becoming unusually chilly at night.

'It was far from winter; in fact the temperatures hover around the mid-twenties during the monsoons, so there was no reason for the staff to complain of cold. However, after repeated complaints, I had them switch their rooms with other staff members.'

After a few days, the other staff also started making similar complaints. My friend thought that this was a pretence by the staff and decided to stay overnight in that room to prove that there was nothing amiss.

'I went to the room and soon fell asleep. However, in the dead of night, I was roused, feeling cold and miserable. It was as if an icy breeze had permeated the room. I checked the windows, but all of them were firmly shut,' Vipin recounted, a palpable strain appearing on his countenance.

'This room is located in the corner of the property and the dampness of the rivulet was causing the chill,' he reasoned to himself.

The next day, that room was promptly closed and the two staff were adjusted in other rooms.

Sometime later, one of the owners came over and stayed at Richmond. He took the corner room on the third floor. That room was also located at the edge of the hotel, right above the staff room in which Vipin and the others had felt the unusual chill.

'I was on night duty—simply dozing off at the reception—when I heard a loud shout from the owner!'

'*O puttar, ey ki ho riya; ye awaaz kittho nu aa rahi* (Oh son, what is happening; from where is this sound coming)?'

The owner was screaming loudly in Punjabi.

As Vipin rushed to the owner's aid, the scared owner had already dashed out of his room, and almost collided with Vipin in the hallway. The middle-aged Punjabi owner, who was otherwise quite loud and dominating, looked like a scared cat.

'*Kuch hora si! Ajeeb awaaaz aa rahi hai kamre ke niche se* (Something is happening! There are strange shouts coming from below the room),' the owner shouted in panic. '*Koi madad ke liye pukar riya si* (Someone is calling for help). "Help-help" *ki cheekh sunai pad rahi hai puttar* (Son, I can hear someone shouting "help-help"),' he added.

A perplexed and frightened Vipin went to the owner's room but could not hear anything. He offered to shift the owner to another room but the owner steadfastly refused and insisted on spending the night on a couch in the lobby.

'I was somewhat amused by the owner's distress and thought that he must have had a nightmare,' Vipin said with a smile.

The owner promptly packed his bags and marched off the next morning, and my friend never saw this person again during his stint at the hotel.

But bizarre occurrences continued to unfold with unsettling frequency, as if some ancient curse had been unleashed.

One night, Vipin and his entire staff were abruptly awoken from their slumber as the 'clip-clop' of a horse's hooves resonated beneath their rooms. All of them, including my friend, rushed out of their rooms in panic and stood speechless as the sound intensified into a crescendo of hoofbeats, until it halted abruptly, leaving behind an eerie silence.

A long silence prevailed as they gathered their wits. 'How can there be a horse below our rooms?' They shouted in panic.

'There is definitely a ghost around! Even the owner had heard strange sounds,' one of them declared, voicing the collective dread.

Vipin somehow managed to console the terrified staff. 'The sound must be coming from the road,' he said. 'Don't panic, go back to sleep.' But most of the staff refused to go back to their rooms. In the morning, five people demanded their dues. Vipin tried his utmost to convince them to stay and even offered a raise.

'This building is haunted. We will not stay even if you double our salaries,' they declared, collected their pending dues and promptly marched off with their bags.

'Already I was trying to come to terms with the scare caused by the strange sounds, and this came as a major setback,' Vipin recalled.

He tried desperately to hire new staff, but those already working in Mussoorie were not willing to work at the Richmond Hotel. And he could not find any more unemployed friends from his native village.

'The owners had to double the salaries of the remaining staff to persuade them to stay. Since it was off-season, we thought we would be able to manage with the diminished staff.'

A few days passed peacefully, until one night a couple staying in a corner room on the first floor called the reception at night. Incidentally, Vipin was manning the night shift once again and the shrill ringing of the phone jolted him awake. Groggily he glanced at the clock—its hands pointed precisely to midnight.

'What could *possibly* be the matter at this ungodly hour?' He grumbled as he reached for the receiver.

'There is a ghost! We can hear a strange voice. Come to our room immediately,' the panic-stricken man shouted.

Once again, Vipin had to rush to the tourist's room. He found the couple standing outside—the scantily clad lady clinging to her husband in panic.

'We heard cries of "help-help" emanating from below our room. It was as if someone was in great distress,' the husband explained. But they steadfastly refused to re-enter the room when Vipin proposed to examine the source of the noise.

'Ok, wait outside the door and do not move away,' Vipin instructed, mustering the courage to step inside, all the while quivering with apprehension. Similar to the previous occurrence in the owner's quarters, Vipin found the room silent, devoid of the distressing sounds that he had been alerted to.

The scared tourists sat in the hotel lobby the entire night and rushed off early next morning, never to return again.

Although, Vipin did not want to tell his staff about this incident—for fear of the remaining ones also leaving—they came to know about it anyway. The scared couple had blurted out everything while having their morning tea!

Yet again there was mutiny among the ranks, with a majority of the remaining staff wanting to quit the job. But Vipin was able to calm them down. 'No one has seen a ghost, apart from the clopping sound. We have not heard any cries of "help" either. So why leave a well-paying job?' he reasoned.

But for good measure, it was decided that a pandit would be called to perform puja to ward off the evil. Pandit-ji did his due, collected a hefty *dakshina* and walked off. The next week was uneventful and it seemed that the evil had truly been contained!

But Vipin was wrong.

One night, Kuldeep—his assistant who managed the front office with him—was on night duty. There wasn't much work and he was passing his time watching an old Hindi movie. When the movie ended, Kuldeep looked at the clock and saw that it was past 1.00 a.m. He was about to take a nap when he heard the 'clip-clop' of a horse's hooves. This time the sound was not coming from down below but from the road behind the reception.

Kuldeep was a brave young man, perhaps the bravest of all the staff. Although he was scared, he mustered enough courage to glance back out of the window of the reception. And yes, he saw a man riding a horse down the road.

As the horse drew near the hotel gate, Kuldeep noticed that the horse rider had an extremely pale face. His head was covered with a felt hat and he wore a coat and a pant.

'Thank God, this is not a ghost,' he muttered to himself.

As the horse rider came to the gate of the hotel, near the rivulet, he and the horse suddenly disappeared into thin air. The sound of the hooves ceased immediately and there was an eerie silence.

Kuldeep was paralyzed with fear. His wide-eyed gaze remained fixated on the darkness beyond. The air felt charged with an otherworldly tension and every nerve in his body screamed for him to flee, but his legs remained rooted to the ground as if bound by invisible chains.

Finally, he came out of his reverie and tried to scream. Only a muffled groan escaped his lips. In sheer panic, he sprinted down to Vipin's room and pounded on the door. As it swung open, Kuldeep let out a shriek, but Vipin was swift enough to muffle it by firmly clasping Kuldeep's mouth with his hand.

'I did not want any more hysterical scenes, so I pulled Kuldeep inside my room and firmly bolted the door before releasing my grip,' Vipin explained.

Kuldeep's terrified face was drained of colour; his lips were pulled back in a painful grimace and beads of sweat had accumulated on his forehead. It took several minutes before the poor man could speak. His sobs rendered his words almost unintelligible. With great effort he managed to narrate the spine-chilling incident. With tears streaming down his face, he uttered, 'I want to go home. I cannot work here.'

Vipin spent the entire night tossing and turning. He

kept wondering if there was an actual evil presence in the hotel. He had definitely heard the sound of horse hooves and felt the unsettling chill in the staff quarters. Yet, doubt gnawed at him: could these eerie occurrences truly be the work of ghosts?

As for the desperate cries for help, Vipin hadn't heard them himself. Kuldeep's account of a vanishing horse and rider left room for scepticism—perhaps the mist and darkness had deceived him.

'Do I have sufficient reason to leave a good job and run away?' He pondered over the matter and finally decided to stay put until he was sure.

Early next morning, he went outside the hotel and closely examined the rivulet that was passing underneath the gate of the hotel to check if indeed a man had fallen down. But there were no such signs.

'The veil of darkness and the swirling monsoon mist must have played tricks on Kuldeep's mind,' he muttered as he retreated to the hotel.

In a bid to douse the matter, Vipin told everyone that Kuldeep's father was unwell and he was going to the village to look after him.

In the ensuing weeks, every nocturnal sound, every guest's voice, and even the boisterous chatter of the staff would send Vipin's heart racing. But thankfully, there were no more scares.

As September approached, tourist arrivals dipped significantly and Vipin had a little more time to himself. He started a routine of going on solitary walks along the

Mall Road. Being a recent immigrant to Mussoorie, he did not know many people here except a few from his village who were also working in various hotels.

One evening, he bumped into Rajesh, a childhood friend from his native village. Rajesh was surprised to find Vipin in Mussoorie. After the usual greetings he asked, 'What brings you to Mussoorie, brother?'

'I am working here in Richmond Hotel.'

'Oh really!' Rajesh looked surprised. 'Since when? Are you alright?'

'Since March this year. But why are you surprised?' Vipin asked, his eyebrows raised.

'Brother, that hotel is haunted. Nobody wants to work there. I would advise you to leave immediately. I will find you another job.'

'How do you know it is haunted, brother? Tell me.'

Rajesh leaned in—his voice hushed and eyes darting around—to ensure no one else overheard him. 'Brother,' he whispered, 'there are many stories of strange events and strange sightings at Richmond. People hear cries and hoof beats, while a few have even seen a ghost!'

'Evil,' Rajesh warned, 'lurks within those walls. Leave Richmond before it ensnares you.'

Reluctantly, Vipin bid adieu to Rajesh and retraced his steps towards Richmond. His scepticism wavered as Rajesh's words hung in the air, mingling with the mist that clung to Mussoorie's hills.

The events of the past few months suddenly seemed more tangible. He felt a sense of dread as he walked into the hotel premises. 'Something is amiss and I have been foolish enough to ignore it. I need to be more careful,' he decided.

Then it happened.

It was a Friday night. Vipin still remembers the day clearly as earlier in the evening he had watched the superhit song 'Roja jaaneman' from the film *Roja* for the first time on *Chitrahaar*. The catchy tune stuck to his lips and he continued to hum the song as he retired to his room.

'It was 12.30 a.m. when I returned to my room, and was changing my clothes when a painful cry of "help" pierced the silence,' Vipin recalled.

His eyes fixated on the wall behind me as he paused the narration.

'What happened then?' I asked eagerly.

He looked at me and let out a deep sigh.

'At first, I dismissed it as my imagination. But the cry repeated again and again. Panic gripped me and I rushed out of my room.

'The bone-chilling cry—desperate and imploring— seemed to echo through the entire basement,' Vipin shuddered. 'One by one, my staff rushed out of their rooms, wide-eyed and trembling, their fear palpable.'

Vipin recalled that the shouts of 'help' had a distinct English accent. 'I knew little English then, but it was unmistakably an Englishman who was pleading for help.'

Everyone rushed up the stairs to the lobby, when the cries ceased.

The terrified group arranged some blankets from the

rooms on the top floor and huddled on the sofas in the dimly lit lobby, trembling and sobbing. Vipin nervously settled on his customary chair behind the reception desk.

Conversations were hushed, punctuated by nervous glances at the staircase. Some speculated about the ghostly cries—it was an Englishman, they all agreed—while others recited prayers under their breath.

After a couple of hours, everyone fell into a nervous slumber and an eerie stillness took over, occasionally broken by the rhythmic snores of a few staff members. The moon's feeble glow filtered through the windows and cast long, dancing shadows across the lobby walls.

It was as if the hotel itself held its breath, waiting for something unseen to unfold.

Vipin, with his feet upon the desk, had briefly dozed off, when a pack of street dogs—dark silhouettes against the moonlit road—started howling outside, as if in warning. Vipin jolted upright and groggily looked at his watch. It was 2.00 a.m.

The crescendo of howls intensified, echoing through the night. Vipin's heart fluttered as he remembered the old superstitions of his village. 'Dogs,' the elders said, 'can sense supernatural presence.'

He glanced through the window of the lobby, trying to discern whether the dogs were gathered outside the hotel gate. The scene outside almost stopped his heartbeat.

'I saw a white man—wearing a broad-brimmed hat and a coat, with trousers tucked into long riding boots— riding a horse towards the hotel,' Vipin recollected.

He stared helplessly—completely paralyzed in fear—
as the ghostly figure on horseback slowly approached
Richmond's gate. 'My mind went blank. I think the
howling of dogs had also stopped as this spectre
approached,' he added.

Just as the rider reached the gate, he suddenly
disappeared into thin air.

'It was as if he never existed,' Vipin's voice trembled.
'But believe me, I was not imagining things. His memory
is still quite vivid in my mind.'

He knew then that it was all over. No amount of
money would persuade him to stay in this haunted place
any longer.

Next morning, he and the other staff members called
up one of the owners and told him that they were
leaving immediately. The owner asked them to wait a
few days till they could come over to settle their dues,
but everyone refused.

'We will not spend a second longer in this property.
It is haunted,' Vipin declared. 'The staff quickly collected
their belongings and left, handing the keys to a local
person sent by the owners.'

'What happened to the hotel subsequently?' I asked.
'It is still running, I believe.'

Vipin said that after this incident, Richmond Hotel
remained closed for several months. 'The owners
desperately tried to hire new staff—offering much more
than the market wages—but the past and recent incidents

had become public knowledge and nobody wanted to work there.'

Eventually, the owners summoned a renowned *tantrik* to dispel the evil. Then they hired staff from New Delhi and restarted the business.

'I am not sure whether the new staff experienced such horrors, but I know for sure that the property was sold off by the Delhi people after a few years,' Vipin said.

The new owner tried his best to run the property—again hiring staff from outside—and stayed at Richmond himself. But it seems that the hotel did not do well and was closed and put up for sale again.

'Maybe the ghost tormented the new owner and his staff too,' Vipin quipped.

This time it was purchased by some businessmen from Lucknow. These people tried to run the property themselves, but financial losses plagued them. Eventually they resorted to leasing it out, but it seems that every person who took the property on lease made heavy losses—perhaps there is still a strong evil lurking in the property.

Subsequent to my conversation with Vipin, I did not meet any other past or present employee of Richmond. But, several years later, I happened to have a conversation with two garrulous elderly gentlemen. I do like to have occasional conversations with the elderly, especially the more talkative ones, as they are able to share rare nuggets of the past.

These gentlemen, who were known to my family, met me in a party at a friend's place. They were sitting in a corner, enjoying their drinks, when I happened to intrude upon them.

It was May and we were experiencing unusual warmth, prompting a conversation about rising temperatures. The old timers opined that lack of snowfall during the winters was one of the reasons for the rising summer temperatures.

I mentioned that I had never seen much snow in the town.

'The maximum snowfall I have witnessed here is around two feet, which was decades ago,' I remarked.

One of the elderly gentlemen began reminiscing about the substantial snowfall during the sixties.

'Boy, you haven't seen real snow then! We have seen four to five feet of snowfall during the sixties. But even that was nothing compared to the eight to ten feet of snowfall in 1945–46 that my father told me about,' said one of the gentlemen while the other nodded in agreement.

'Eight to ten feet of snow is unbelievable! I hope it is not the liquor playing tricks on your minds, sirs,' I teased.

'A few pegs of liquor have never affected our minds! It is true that Mussoorie witnessed eight to ten feet of snow in the winter of 1945. And for your information, the weather was so cold that it snowed even upto Rajpur in Dehradun,' added the second gentleman, a bit peeved.

I apologized to them and said that I was merely

jesting and not doubting their word. Once pacified, the gentleman provided more details about the snowfall.

'My father had told me that as the snow piled up, people resorted to digging deep trenches just to create pathways for walking, and it took over a month for all the snow to melt,' one of them said.

'Food shortages plagued the town since roads remained closed, and survival meant rationing supplies of potatoes, rotis and rice,' the other added.

'Such hardship for the residents; they must have had a horrid time,' I said.

'Yes. Tragically, lives were also lost—some under harrowing circumstances. According to old timers, an English gentleman met a most unfortunate end while riding during the snowstorm. Due to poor visibility his horse plummeted down a gorge. The horse and the rider remained buried in the snow for over a month, until the thaw revealed their lifeless forms,' one of them said.

The body of the rider was apparently found trapped under the horse.

'According to my father, the unfortunate man must have found himself trapped beneath the weight of the fallen steed. Injured, but perhaps still alive, he must have struggled futilely, unable to free himself from the burden that pinned him down,' he added.

'Oh my God!' I gasped. 'Where did this incident take place?'

'He fell in the gorge bordering the present-day Richmond Hotel,' came the reply.

It was as if I had been struck by lightning. Immediately, the cries of 'help', the sound of horse's hooves, and the spectre of the Englishman riding a horse began to make sense.

'The unfortunate man must have ridden down the rivulet, into the gorge below and might have lain there— God knows how long—shouting for help. But who would hear his cries in the snowstorm?' I thought.

'And now he roams around the place, riding his horse on moonlit nights.'

I have no clue whether the spectral rider still canters his horse on moonlit nights, whether the sound of hooves or the man's desperate cries of 'help' still echo in the halls of Richmond. But I do pray to God for the peace of that unfortunate Englishman's soul.

                    ∽

# Cobbler and the Yaksh

Kundan was born in Dehradun, sometime in the 1890s, into a family of cobblers that hailed from the Itawah-Mainpuri region in erstwhile United Province[*].

The British required cobblers to make shoes for the soldiers at the Dehradun cantonment and persuaded able artisans from Itawah-Mainpuri to come to the city. These cobblers were given land to build their houses on what is now Kanwali Road.

Kundan's father Moti Lal was a skilled cobbler who moved to Dehradun around 1880 as a young man and lived in a makeshift shack on Kanwali Road for many years, sharing it with two fellow cobblers from his hometown. Moti Lal was able to find brisk business as the Dehradun cantonment was expanding and his boots came in great demand. After a few years, Moti Lal had saved enough money to build a house and marry a woman from his native village.

Kundan, the firstborn, inherited his physical traits from his mother—particularly her fair complexion and

---

*Present-day Uttar Pradesh

dark eyes. As Moti Lal worked tirelessly—making boots in one corner of their modest one-room house—young Kundan sat by his side for hours and watched him cut leather, stitch boots, and polish them to a high shine. The boy rather enjoyed the scent of leather and polish that permeated his house.

He started assisting his father from a very young age. He began by polishing the shoes assembled by Moti Lal and urged him to teach him to cut and stitch leather. In a few years, Kundan had mastered the art of cutting and stitching, preparing inner and outer soles, skilfully attaching them to the upper leather, and meticulously finishing and polishing each shoe to perfection.

'You have a knack for perfection and a keen eye for detail. You will become a gifted shoemaker,' Moti Lal would often encourage Kundan while teaching him the intricacies of shoemaking. Being praised by his father would fill Kundan with immense joy.

'I want to make a name as the best shoemaker in the country. I want every soldier and every gora saheb to wear my shoes,' Kundan would often say to himself. He dreamt of owning a big shop where a number of apprentices would prepare shoes while he attended to the gora sahebs coming to give their feet measurements.

But young Kundan's life took a drastic turn when a cholera epidemic broke out and claimed the lives of his parents, leaving him distraught and alone.

'Oh God, why did you spare me? You should have taken me too! How will I live without my parents,' he cried in sorrow as he sat in one corner of his house for several days. Finally—his mind made up—he left home and started walking towards Haridwar.

'I do not want to live. I will jump into the Ganga and end my life,' he muttered as he marched along.

It took Kundan five days to reach Haridwar. The long walk and lack of food had left him utterly exhausted, but he did not stop until he reached the banks of the Ganga.

'O mother, please forgive me for ending my life. Please enfold me in your embrace, mother,' he implored, kneeling at the bank of the river. But due to exhaustion, he was unable to rise and collapsed there.

He lay unconscious on the river bank for several hours. People passed by, looking at him with pity, but no one approached him. Perhaps they thought he was another victim of cholera.

In his unconscious state, Kundan heard his mother's voice.

'Kundan... Kundan... *Wake up...*' The voice urged.

His eyes snapped open, eager to look at the loving face of his mother. But he was alarmed as he realized it was actually the voice of a stranger who was leaning over him and calling his name.

Seeing that Kundan had regained consciousness, the thick lips of the stranger curled into a wide smile, revealing a row of yellow teeth. 'Are you alright, Kundan?' he asked in a low, rumbling voice.

Hearing his name uttered by the stranger made Kundan gasp in surprise, and a shiver ran down his spine. Now fully alert, he cast a searching gaze over the stranger's face, trying to discern any hint of familiarity.

The stranger's face was unusually long, his complexion a rich, dark brown. His weathered skin—marked by fine wrinkles that traced the contours of his face—and the silver hair that fell up to his neck made the man look as old as eternity. Thick, formidable handlebar whiskers framed a mouth that hinted at both mischief and danger. But his most unsettling features were the piercing red eyes that seemed to see into Kundan's soul.

'I have never seen you before. How do you know my name?' Kundan's voice posed more of an accusation than a question, his words tumbling out in a rush of anxiety and confusion.

'Never mind,' said the stranger as he effortlessly hoisted Kundan to his feet with one hand. His touch was like a conduit, transferring a surge of energy through Kundan's weary veins. He felt his fatigue melt away, replaced by a newfound strength and vitality.

As Kundan stood before the stranger, he was surprised by the man's extraordinary height. 'He must be eight or ten feet tall,' Kundan thought. Fear gripped him and he nervously looked around to call someone for help, but found that he and the stranger were enveloped in an isolating fog.

'He is not a human,' Kundan thought to himself. He tried to shout for help but his voice remained trapped in his throat.

'Indeed,' the stranger's voice resonated, 'I am no

mere mortal.' His eyes bore into Kundan's, revealing power and wisdom beyond the ordinary. 'Do not be afraid, Kundan. I am not here to harm you. Had I not intervened, your soul would have left your body by now.'

Kundan was stupefied, his mind filled with fear and curiosity. Even in the biting cold, the stranger was just wearing a half jacket. Both his arms were exposed. Kundan noticed intricate symbols—in some unknown language—etched along both of them. He tried to flee, but his feet remained rooted in place by some invisible force.

'Who are you?' Kundan finally managed to ask in a trembling voice.

'My name is Jaakh. I am a *Yaksh*, disciple of Yamraj. I was meditating on the bank of Maa Ganga, when I sensed your arrival and learnt that you were in great misery. Your soul teetered on the edge of life and death.'

'Why did you intervene?'

Kundan was puzzled. He recalled the darkness that had consumed him, and the ache of loss.

'I was ready to let go…'

Jaakh's enigmatic smile held compassion.

'Not yet,' he declared. 'I know that since you survived today, you will have a long life ahead of you.'

'You must go back and take up the occupation of your father. Destiny has great things in store for you,' Jaakh added.

'But my parents! How can I overcome their loss?' Kundan remonstrated.

'You will learn to live with it. Remember that you have a long life ahead of you to pursue your dream of making shoes for the goras,' Jaakh added with a mischievous smile.

Kundan shuddered. 'Jaakh even knows about my dreams and thoughts,' he thought.

'Yes, I can read your mind and learn everything! Now go back to Dehradun,' Jaakh ordered.

He instructed Kundan to lead a life of honesty and integrity and steer clear of the temptations of wrongdoings.

'If you avoid a sinful life, you shall be blessed with good fortune. But if you do not, you will pay a heavy price,' Jaakh warned, adding that maybe they would meet again.

Kundan bowed at his feet and marched back home with a newfound determination. There, he found his neighbours grieving for him. 'I am well,' he assured them.

From the next day onwards, Kundan got back to completing the few pending orders that his father had secured prior to his untimely death. 'Once I deliver these shoes, the gora sahibs would appreciate my craftsmanship and give me more orders,' he thought joyfully. But when he reached the office of the quartermaster to deliver the shoes, he got a scolding from his assistant.

'You were supposed to deliver these shoes 15 days ago. Go away and never come back again,' he admonished.

With the doors of the Dehradun cantonment closed to him, Kundan stood at the threshold of uncertainty.

For several days he contemplated upon the path ahead. He knew that if he was not able to secure orders from the cantonment, he would be unable to establish his own enterprise.

'O Yaksh! You said that I have a great future, but I think it was a lie,' he muttered with disappointment. That night, as he slept feverishly, Kundan dreamt that he was standing alongside Jaakh at the bank of the Ganga. 'You are a skilled cobbler,' Jaakh said, 'why don't you try getting a job?'

The dream lingered in Kundan's mind. Based on the advice of Jaakh, he diligently searched for a job at the shops of friends and acquaintances of his father and was finally able to secure a job with Ramu *kaka*, a close friend of his father. He welcomed Kundan into his workshop, where several apprentices worked. The air smelled of leather and polish, and the rhythmic tapping of hammers against shoe soles filled the room.

For the next four years, Kundan worked tirelessly under the watchful eyes and guidance of Ramu kaka. He was an excellent mentor and patiently shared the secrets of the craft, revealing the subtle nuances that transformed raw materials into finely crafted footwear. Once Ramu kaka granted a two-day leave to his apprentices and they seized the opportunity to explore the nearby town of Mansuri[*]. With great excitement, they hired a carriage from their workshop on Kanwali Road to Rajpur. From

---

*Present-day Mussoorie

Rajpur, they undertook a seven-mile climb to reach the picturesque settlement of Mansuri.

Kundan was enamoured by the beauty and salubrious climate of this town.

'It would be great to live and work here, amidst such pleasing vistas,' he thought, his gaze tracing the winding paths that disappeared into the oak forests.

The group spent one night at Mansuri, staying at a cheap lodge in Landour where Kundan learnt of a cantonment located there, hidden amidst the serene landscape. Having been turned away from the Dehradun cantonment, Kundan's thoughts turned to the potential for cobbling work at the Landour cantonment—especially since he found very few cobblers around.

Kundan scouted the handful of cobblers around Landour and Mansuri, engaging in conversations to understand the scope of work in the town. He found that despite the limited regimental presence, there was sufficient demand from army personnel, as well as from visitors who thronged the town during summer. This revelation sparked a flicker of opportunity in Kundan's mind. 'What better than to set up shop here amidst the cool climes,' he thought. The whispering oak trees seemed to nod in agreement, as if welcoming him to their fold.

That night, he thought of Jaakh and prayed to him to guide him for his future. Yet again, Jaakh appeared in his dreams, standing at the same spot where Kundan had met him. 'Kundan, do not be afraid of new challenges. Do what your heart says,' he advised.

Once the seed of ambition had taken root within Kundan, he set after his dream with unwavering determination. Over the next year Kundan toiled tirelessly, saving every penny he earned. He also made a quick trip to Mansuri to work out the logistics, selected a small shop on the Mullingar slope and gave advance to the owner for the next season.

The next March, he bid farewell to Ramu kaka, who was none too pleased to let him go but wished him well nonetheless and promised to support him in his endeavours.

'Boy, if you receive a large order, I can send an apprentice or two to assist you,' he assured him.

Kundan already had his father's tools and equipments which he carried across the hills, dreaming of a new beginning. There was a flutter of anticipation in his stomach as his future appeared as obscured as Mansuri veiled by the morning mist.

After setting up his shop at Landour, Kundan faced the challenge of attracting clients. The breakthrough came when one Welsh teacher from Woodstock School saw the young man sitting idle in his shop and—taking pity on him—ordered a pair of shoes. The craftsman that he was, Kundan put his heart and soul into making a pair that delighted the Welshman, who recommended him to the entire Woodstock staff.

As luck would have it, on Sundays the teacher used to play poker with the commandant of Landour cantonment and put in a word about Kundan with him as well.

This was the turning point of his life, and soon his reputation for stitching comfortable and sturdy shoes spread across the town. His once quiet and deserted shop now thrummed with the footsteps of gora sahebs, making Kundan's dreams a reality. Soon Kundan got orders to make shoes for the soldiers posted at Landour cantonment and he had to hire apprentices to work for him.

By 1920, Kundan had opened two shops, one in Landour and another one close to where the hotel Whispering Windows stands today. As the number of apprentices increased, he also opened a workshop at Barlowgunj where the shoes were stitched.

By now he was a wealthy man, and with riches came vices. He took to alcohol and started drinking heavily—there were days when he was already drunk by afternoon. Kundan's generosity helped him make many friends, but many of them were eyeing his wealth. Such opportunists—who used to make merry at Kundan's expense—also allured him into attending *mujra*s and taking up gambling.

Every evening, after closing his shop, Kundan would summon a horse-drawn carriage—his preferred mode of travel through the narrow lanes of Landour—to reach the mujra and gambling dens. He carried sacks full of coins and notes to gamble away or shower upon the dancing girls. He would return in the quiet hours before dawn—a heavy odour of liquor on his breath and the cheap perfume of nautch girls lingering on his clothes. His money-filled sacks would be invariably empty.

By the time he reached home, his wife Kanta would be fast asleep. She had started sleeping in a separate room and no longer waited for Kundan, after he refused to change despite her repeated remonstrations.

Not only was Kundan losing money heavily, his business was also being affected.

'I had ordered my shoes two weeks ago but till now you have been unable to deliver, and I have to leave for Dilli now,' admonished one gentleman.

Due to Kundan's lack of attention to work, he was unable to complete orders on time and many of his apprentices had taken to moonlighting surreptitiously. But these things did not matter to Kundan as his newly acquired wealth had made him extremely haughty.

'O, I have lots of wealth. I don't care about losing a little on gambling. As for my customers, they cannot go anywhere, no one can make shoes like I do,' he would proclaim whenever any well-wisher tried to talk some sense into him.

One night, as Kundan was in a deep sleep, he dreamt that he had died and was standing in a long queue at the gates of hell. Jaakh was standing at the gate and pushing people inside. Kundan could hear cries of agony coming from within. 'These must be the shouts of souls getting punished,' he thought with a chill.

The unbearable heat emanating from hell was debilitating. Kundan could barely lift his feet as he moved forward in the queue. Finally, after what felt like an eternity, Kundan reached the gate to hell. He called out Jaakh's name, hoping to catch his attention amidst the chaos, who swiftly approached Kundan upon hearing him. With a voice as coarse as gravel, he uttered, 'Kundan, I warned you to stay away from the path of sin, yet you turned a deaf ear. Now, the time has come for you to bear the consequences.' Saying this, Jaakh pushed him into hell. 'No, please forgive me! I will do as you said,' Kundan shouted and awoke with a jolt, drenched in cold sweat.

He tried to rise from the bed to drink some water but found that he could not move a muscle.

With a lot of effort, he tried again but was able to lift neither his feet nor his hands. He tried to shout for help but could barely manage a quake. Kundan fruitlessly attempted to rise from the bed again. Desperation clawed at his throat as the room seemed to close in and the air thickened with dread.

When Kanta came to his room in the morning, she found Kundan rooted to his bed and tears of sorrow flowing through his eyes. He tried desperately to speak to his wife—he wanted to apologize for hurting her, to promise that he would change—but was only able to mutter incoherently. But Kanta understood and held his hand, her own tears mirroring his—a silent testament that she shared Kundan's pain.

In the months that followed, Kanta's dedication to her husband's care was unwavering. She tended to Kundan with the same attentiveness and affection one would give to a child.

Meanwhile, lying helplessly on his bed, Kundan spent his days and nights praying to God, seeking divine forgiveness and pleading with Jaakh for mercy. He made solemn promises to mend his ways and commit himself to charity. After several months of illness, Kundan showed signs of improvement. He was able to move his fingers and speak in monosyllables, which Kanta understood.

Finally, almost a year since he was bedridden, Kundan managed to get up with Kanta's support. As his eyes brimmed with tears of joy, Kundan profusely thanked his maker and also Jaakh for blessing him to get back on his feet.

It was nothing short of a miracle that Kundan recovered completely within a few more months. Now he was a transformed man. He gave up drinking, gambling and going to the seedy dens of the nautch girls. He started giving more time to his work, became polite towards his customers and staff, and his business was soon back on track. He worked tirelessly and managed to gain inroads into Meerut cantonment, where a large deployment of soldiers meant that he started getting sizeable orders.

He and Kanta were extremely happy and spent a lot of time together, their joy not diminished by the absence of an offspring.

All was well until, one evening, Kundan bumped into his old friend Ram Ashish on Mall Road.

'My friend, how are you? Seems you have given up on old friends,' Ram Ashish said.

'No, my friend, how can I forget you! It's just that I have been very busy with my work,' Kundan replied sheepishly.

'Then come with me. We are having a party at my house,' Ram Ashish invited. Kundan tried his best to avoid going to the party, but his friend was insistent and he finally gave in.

'Here, Kundan, have a glass of rum for old times' sake,' Ram Ashish said and set the glass before him. Initially, Kundan refused to drink. But all his friends gathered at the party kept insisting and he reluctantly picked up the glass.

This signalled the death knell for his cobbling business.

After this evening, Kundan started meeting his old 'friends' frequently and was surrounded by a motley crew who—being aware of Kundan's benevolent nature—wanted to make merry at his expense. Soon he took to his old ways again—drinking, gambling and visiting the nautch girls. Once again, he stopped paying attention to his business and started getting complaints from customers, while his apprentices started stealing from him. Like earlier times, every evening he returned home way past midnight, heavily drunk.

Kanta tried everything to persuade Kundan into mending his ways—she cajoled him, snapped at him, shouted at him and even threatened to leave him—but to no avail. Kundan was not only heavily influenced by his friends but also enjoying the revelry.

In his merrymaking, he seemed to have forgotten all about his promises to Jaakh. One evening, while returning after meeting a friend on Camel's Back Road, Kundan took a shortcut through Lavender Lane (Tar Gali as it is called now)—the narrow and steep path connecting the desolate Camel's Back Road with the bustling Mall Road. He was smiling to himself, thinking about the nautch girls and their promises for the evening, when he noticed a huge dark shadow stretched across the gravel path.

Kundan's footsteps faltered and his heart quickened.

What could cast such an imposing silhouette in the fading light?

As he gazed at the source of the shadow, he heard it call out his name.

'Kundan,' the shadow rasped, its voice like wind through barren branches. 'You have strayed far from your path.'

'Jaakh,' exclaimed Kundan, the name escaping his lips like an ominous whisper.

The figure stepped forward, emerging from the shadows just enough for Kundan to recognize the familiar, sinister face.

'Yes, it's me,' Jaakh's voice cut through the silence like a blade. 'Seems like you're not happy to see me?' There was a hint of amusement in his tone, a cruel satisfaction at Kundan's discomfort.

His throat tightened.

'I... I am...so happy...to see you, sir,' he stammered, the words feeling foreign and insincere even as they left his lips.

'No, you are not,' Jaakh boomed, his sarcastic smile now replaced by a cold, hard stare that pierced through Kundan's soul. 'I gave you a new life and asked you to pursue the path of good. But you have broken your promise repeatedly.' The accusation was tinged with disappointment.

Kundan felt as if he had been lifted from the familiar cobblestones of Lavender Lane into the clouds. A kaleidoscope of his past played out before his eyes— the reckless gambling, the drunken revelry, the seductive dances of the nautch girls. Each image flashed by, reminding him of the sins he had committed and the promises he had broken.

He realized that he had wandered far from the path he once knew, chasing after immoral desires. Jaakh had granted him a second chance—a chance to redeem himself—and Kundan had squandered it.

The wind blew through the oak trees in foreboding whispers.

Kundan fell to his knees, tears streaming down his face. 'Forgive me,' he wept in a barely audible voice, 'I lost my way.'

'You had your chances,' Jaakh said, his voice low and cold. 'But now it's time to face the consequences of your actions.'

Kundan trembled with fear and knelt before him with folded hands.

'Don't be scared. I am not going to end your life. In fact, I will grant you a very long life,' Jaakh roared. Kundan looked curiously at Jaakh, not sure what he meant. His heart raced, torn between fear and curiosity.

What kind of bargain was this?

An evil grin spread across Jaakh's countenance. 'But I will make sure that from now on, you will spend your life repenting every sin and every misdeed that you have committed.' The words hung in the air like a curse, heavy and suffocating.

'Your life will be devoid of any kind of happiness,' Jaakh continued, 'you will lose everything you have and wander around burdened by remorse.'

Before he could respond, Jaakh disappeared, leaving Kundan lying prostrate on the cold ground, sobbing inconsolably.

A few months elapsed since Kundan's meeting with Jaakh. He was beginning to think that it was a bad dream and had started believing that nothing would happen, until tragedy struck one day. While hanging clothes out to dry, Kanta slipped off a cliff bordering Kundan's house, fell into the gorge below and lost her life.

Kundan was crestfallen, especially since he had no children.

'I am once again left all alone in this world,' he would mutter aloud, his words a testament to the profound void left by Kanta's absence. He was now sure that Jaakh's warning would ring true.

A short time later, World War II broke out and Kundan's already dwindling business took another hit. The British government's spending cuts had a domino effect—orders were cancelled and debts mounted. Kundan's once-thriving enterprise now teetered on the edge of collapse. One by one, he had to sell off each of his shops to meet the mounting debts, until he was only left with the shop-cum-production facility at Landour and his house. He also had to cut down his staff until there was only one apprentice left.

A short while after World War II, as Kundan was trying to somehow reestablish his lost business, India's independence was announced. Apart from the army, Kundan also catered to European clients. But the mass exodus of all foreign nationals meant that his client base was completely eroded.

He was forced to sell his shop at Landour, let go of his only apprentice and also sell his house. His opportunist friends—who used to make merry at Kundan's expense—turned their backs on Kundan.

The great cobbler, once regarded as being among the wealthiest people of Mansuri, was now a pauper who lived in a tiny one-room shack behind Mullingar.

It was in early 1980 when an old man appeared at our doorstep. He carried his age with a grace that defied mere years.

He had long silver hair that hid his ears and fell upon his face. His face, etched by time, bore the map of a life fully lived. The man's eyes were like ancient wells, holding depths that were difficult to fathom, covered by thick unruly brows that resembled overgrown bushes. His forehead was lined with deep furrows that bore witness to a troubled past.

The man wore a long overcoat that spoke of better days long past—it had been mended so many times that it was difficult to make out the original material. But his shoes defied time and gleamed as if freshly crafted.

Despite his haggard appearance, the man stood proudly with a stature that seemed to command respect.

'Child, is your grandfather at home?'

'Yes, he is. Let me call him,' I replied.

My grandfather, a jovial and pleasant person, greeted the man with familiarity and cordially called him inside.

'Come, Kundan,' my grandfather said, gesturing toward the worn-out armchair. But Kundan shook his head. 'No need for that, *babuji*. I'm more comfortable here.' And he settled on his haunches upon the floor.

'He is Kundan—one of the best cobblers in the country. The shoes that you are wearing have been crafted by him,' my grandfather introduced me to the man.

'Child, my shoes will not tear, their sole will not break. They will last until you outgrow them,' Kundan added like a polished salesman.

As I moved away to watch television, they chatted for

a while. A little later I noticed my grandfather putting some money into Kundan's palm, which he accepted gratefully.

From that day onwards, Kundan visited our house once or twice every week and every time grandfather gave him some money. Sometimes my mother would offer him tea and a few *paranthas* which he would gleefully accept, his eyes crinkling with gratitude.

'Why do you always give him money?' I asked grandfather one day.

'Kundan is a good man and an old friend. Throughout my life I have been wearing shoes made by him. A very wealthy man once who has met with misfortune,' grandfather said with a deep sigh.

'What happened to him? How was he reduced to such a pitiable state?' I enquired.

'Son, next time he comes, you can ask him yourself,' grandfather replied.

I waited eagerly for the cobbler's next visit, which was luckily on a Sunday when I was home. I paced around impatiently until Kundan settled on the floor in his customary style. Sensing my eagerness, my grandfather said, 'Kundan, my grandson wants to ask a few questions. I hope you won't mind.'

'Babuji, I will be happy to talk to your grandson,' Kundan replied.

Gathering my courage, I approached the cobbler and said, 'Uncle, grandfather tells me you were once a wealthy man. What happened to change your fortunes?'

'Ah, young one, it's a long story,' Kundan looked up at me with a faint smile. 'But if you have the time, I will share it with you. Meanwhile, can you ask your mother to please make a cup of tea for me?'

That is how I learnt Kundan's life story. I realized that he not only had a razor-sharp memory but was also a great storyteller. For hours—over several cups of tea and one round of paranthas—he unravelled the threads of his past, revealing every intricate detail.

'So how old are you now?' I enquired.

'I have crossed 90,' was the reply.

'How long a life has the Yaksh promised you?'

My curiosity was piqued.

There was a long pause. Kundan seemed a bit nervous now.

'I... I do not know,' he stammered nervously, 'but Jaakh said that he would meet me one more time and only then my salvation would be possible. I have been waiting for Jaakh for many decades. I do not want to live this lonely and sad life much longer.'

Kundan was crying, his trembling hands covering his face. My eyes were moist, and as I glanced at my grandfather, I noticed tears in his eyes as well.

Sensing the tension building up, grandfather invited Kundan to stay back for lunch. He nodded gratefully and wiped away his tears.

Kundan continued to come to our house for several years. By now we had become quite friendly, and I would often ask him, 'Did Jaakh come to meet you?'

Every time, he would shake his head in the negative.

After a few years, he stopped coming to our house. 'Maybe Kundan is unwell,' grandfather reasoned.

I did not see him again. One evening, grandfather informed me that Kundan had passed away.

Had Jaakh come to meet him one last time? Did he relieve Kundan of his loneliness and sad life? Was he absolved of his sins?

These are some questions that will remain unanswered!

# Acknowledgements

Writing this book has been a journey made possible by the support of many remarkable individuals. I owe them all a deep debt of gratitude.

First and foremost, I remember my grandfather and father, who lived their lives rooted in the hills of Mussoorie. They knew its people, its whispers, and its strange, unforgettable tales. Both of them are no longer with me, but I am sure they must be smiling from above as I remember them.

To my wonderful wife, Neha, I owe endless thanks. She has been my support and inspiration throughout this process—urging me to open my laptop during bouts of writer's block. She provided invaluable feedback on early drafts, keeping me motivated with her unwavering belief in me. My nephew, Vinayak, also played a vital role, reading each story with care and suggesting thoughtful improvements.

A special mention goes to my son, Anant, whose enthusiasm lit up every conversation about this book. His mature insights—on everything from feedback about the stories, story titles, to the book's cover design—shaped this work in ways I couldn't have imagined. Without his support I may have never been able to write this book.

I am grateful to the legend Mr Ruskin Bond for his generous endorsement. I am deeply humbled by his kind words and I've learnt he's been eagerly awaiting the book's release in print.

I also extend my heartfelt thanks to Mr Victor Banerjee, the most affable and down-to-earth filmstar, for the lovely endorsement, and to Mr Bill Aitken for gracing this book with his insightful foreword.

I must also thank Sunil bhaiya of Cambridge Book Depot, whose gentle nudge helped me overcome my initial reluctance to pen down these ghost stories.

My friends Jaiprakash Uttarakhandi, a distinguished historian and journalist, and Shoorveer Bhandari, another journalist, deserve a word of thanks for sharing real-life incidents.

To all the characters who feature in my book—some named, many unnamed—thank you. Their lives, their mysteries, and the events that unfolded around them are the heartbeat of this book. Without them, these stories would not exist.

Finally, I express my gratitude to the exceptional team at Rupa Publications, particularly Mr Dibakar Ghosh, for their dedication and expertise in bringing this book to life.